THE ST. CROIX CARTEL

MZ. LADY P

The St. Croix Cartel

Copyright © 2019 by Mz. Lady P

Published by Shan Presents
www.shanpresents.com

SUBSCRIBE

Text Shan to 22828 to stay up to date with new releases, sneak peeks, contest, and more....

SUBMISSIONS

**To submit your manuscript to Shan Presents, please
send the first three chapters and synopsis
to submissions@shanpresents.com**

NOTE FROM THE AUTHOR

As you all know every book that I write is filled with a purpose for something greater! Although you may never understand why I do plots the way I do. Trust and believe there is a method to my madness. My madness creates a colorful display of powerful men and women going through the woes of Urban Life! In this book you will see characters from Heaven's life before she married Cross. It's important because even though she has married into the St. Croix family she comes from a powerful family herself. Thank you all for your support and the understanding of the way I plot my books and link them. My books are not for the faint hearted!!! Grab a glass of wine, relax, and get lost in my madness.

WELCOME TO THE ST. CROIX CARTEL

CHAPTER ONE
CROSS

"THIS MUST BE HEAVEN" by Brainstorm played softly in the background as Heaven and I danced for the first time as husband and wife. It felt like we were on top of the clouds looking down at the world. We had come so far in such a short time. It was crazy how motherfuckers had tried everything to keep us apart. All them bitches failed miserably. Right now, in this moment, I'm in heaven, and the shit feels so good. I thought to watch her give birth to my firstborn son was everything, but it wasn't anything compared to officially changing her last name. A nigga was complete. I finally had my own little family. It was us against the world, and anybody could get it if they thought shit was sweet. I get on that gangsta shit with these niggas in the streets, but with Heaven, I'm like putty in her hands, and she doesn't even know it.

Pulling Heaven closer to me, I hummed the words to the song in her ear.

"I love you so much."

"A nigga love you too, Mrs. St Croix. You know this shit is until the casket drops, right?"

"I wouldn't have it any other way." We engaged in another kiss and continued to dance.

Although the room was filled to capacity, in that moment, it was only my wife and me. That was until we heard some commotion coming from the back of the room. Looking up I saw the nigga Lil Dro fighting with security. This nigga was so ready to get a bullet put in his head. I've literally scheduled a sit-down with his people behind this nigga thinking he could shoot me and continue breathing. He had only lasted this long out of respect for Heaven and their daughter. I intended to kill this nigga, but I couldn't do it until after she gave birth to my seed. The whole pregnancy she was afraid the baby would die during birth, so I had to do everything in my power to keep her calm. That's the only reason murking this fuck nigga had been placed on the backburner. That added with the fact that I had business dealings with his people, but them niggas had no control over his ass. Fuck business at this point. This fuck nigga has been making this shit personal. I'm done playing!

Pulling the gun from the holster that I had on beneath my suit jacket, I snatched away from Heaven and headed towards him.

"Noooo Crosss!"

Heaven tried her best to hold me, but she wasn't strong enough. This nigga Lil Dro was attempting to ruin our wedding day, so it was nothing that could save his ass at this point!"

"Say the word bro, and we can send this bitch to the moon!" Priest was right there with his gold AK.

"You niggas know I'm down for a good gun fight!" Saint was right beside me with Helen— that was the name he gave his chopper. The nigga never left home without it. We were like one band one fucking sound at the moment. My father not shit these days, but he taught us to be trained to go.

We headed in his direction, and that's when the whole Legacy Inc. stood up with their shit out. The big homies Remy, Thug, and Malik were trying to contain the situation. They couldn't do shit with a crew of young wild ass niggas. Besides my brothers, my street team was locked and motherfucking loaded.

"Let's send this hoe up then!" Kaine yelled as he upped his shit.

A shot was let off, and it was pandemonium from there. It sounded like the Fourth of July in this bitch. As I let off shots, I realized we were being ambushed. We had been infiltrated. The niggas that were waiters was shooting at both Thug Legacy Inc. and the St. Croix Cartel.

Laid out on the floor shooting, I was in shock looking at the bitches shooting and fucking the waiters up. Right now was not the time, but my dick was hard as fuck. My wife should not be standing on top of a table in her eighty thousand dollar wedding gown on her wedding day handling a Mac-10 like a nigga. When the smoke cleared, the waiters were laid out. It was a motherfucking massacre. Bodies were everywhere. I had lost some niggas on my street team, and so did Legacy Inc. As the smell of gunpowder permeated the air, I was glad the kids were sent home after the wedding.

Once the smoke cleared, I was glad to see all of our people made it out alive, but now we had a bigger issue to deal with. Who the fuck was these niggas and who sent them? They had literally been sent on a dummy mission because they were all dead.

"I can't believe they ruined my wedding day!"

"Stop crying, babe! The most important thing we were able to say I do before that shit kicked off. This shit could be worse. We could have lost our people, but by the grace of God, we didn't. Stop crying. I'm about to head out to this meeting with your people. We were all being shot at. There's a beef somewhere, and we need to find out where the fuck it's coming from. Plus, I'm still fucking your bitch ass baby daddy up!"

"Just forget it, Cross. Please don't go. Let's just go on our honeymoon." Heaven was all emotional and shit. I needed her to stop this quick.

"Come here and wipe your face! Earlier today, I watched you boss the fuck up, so the tears I see are unacceptable. You know I have to handle this shit. If we were to go on our honeymoon, we would still have to come home to unfinished business. We have the rest of our life to travel all over the fucking world. Do you trust me, Mrs. St. Croix?" I lifted her chin so that she could look at me in my eyes.

"Yes! I trust you. Please hurry up back. I'm not going to be able to sleep or anything until you make it back home to me."

"I want you to remember something. I'll always come back to you."

We engaged in a long passionate kiss before I walked out of our penthouse suite at Trump Tower in downtown Chicago. As I hopped on the elevator and met up with my people in the lobby, I felt like shit. My baby's wedding day was ruined, and somebody got to pay for that shit with their life. I wasn't even twenty-four hours into this marriage thing, and a bitch was trying me.

━━━

"Bro, you sure about these motherfuckers?" Priest asked as he placed the magazine in his gun.

"That's the same shit I'm trying to see. For all we know them niggas could have set that shit up," Saint spoke as he blew smoke from his cigarette.

I wanted to knock his big ass out because he knows I hate him to smoke that shit in my car.

"Trust me. The only nigga in this bitch that's on bullshit is this motherfucker Dro. He is doing all this shit behind some pussy. His crew be on some business shit. At the same time, they all go hard for each other just like we do. This shit is business and personal as fuck. I know that nigga hit me up, and I'm not letting that shit just go like that. This shit puts Heaven in the middle of a bunch of bullshit, and she done been through enough." I flamed up a blunt and passed it to Priest.

"Now, I fucks with Heaven, don't get me wrong. How do you

know she won't turn on you for them? I mean let's keep this shit one hundred. She's married to you, but she grew up with them."

"Did you see my baby bussing that Mac today, my nigga? My wife is riding with me one hundred percent. Make that the last time you question her intentions."

"Your ass is sprung as fuck on Heaven, lil bro," Saint said being funny but wasn't shit funny. This is the same man who cried like a bitch at his wedding ceremony. It doesn't get anymore sprung than that.

"Let's get in here and handle this shit. We have shit to handle back home in the A."

Priest was right. With our father being locked up, we were now in control of everything. I was still doing my shit in Chicago, but I had to go back to Atlanta. It was a St. Croix thing. My brothers needed me more than my business associates in Chicago did. I'm just grateful my wife is moving with me. I know it's going to be a hard transition for her, and I was going to make sure I made the transition as smooth as possible.

We all hopped out of the car and walked inside of the Legacy Inc. Headquarters. I had no issue with meeting in their territory. Lil Ace and Amari were already sitting at the table talking with Remy and his brother Thug. We all still had our suits on and shit. Blunts were being passed around and liquor was flowing. This wasn't a fucking social call for me. I had shit that needs to be addressed.

"Let's get this shit handled. I have a plane to catch!" I sat down at the table and stared at this nigga Dro intensely. My blood was boiling at the moment.

"Why the fuck you going around telling people I shot you? I can assure you it wasn't me because your ass would be dead right now!"

"Pipe the fuck down! You're the only nigga that had a motive. I'm not beefing with nobody out here. You the only person walking around pressed because Heaven is with me. Then you show up today on bullshit. Not after two minutes of you being there, a big ass gunfight erupts!" I banged my fist against the table out of anger. This nigga was truly trying the fuck out of me.

"Calm down, Cross! We were all there, and it was obvious those waiters were shooting at both sides. My brothers and I are out of the game and have been for years. As for Legacy Inc., I can vouch for all of them and say they had nothing to do with what happened today. I can even take it a step further and show you proof that Lil Dro didn't hit you up. While that shit was going on, he was in Cali securing a deal for the team. The signing of his rights and shit were all a ploy to keep Heaven from being worried. I'll vouch for the nigga on that. This other shit though you and him have to handle that shit as men. As a man that don't play about his wife, I understand your frustration. Lil Dro you know I'm your Big Unc Thug, and I've killed a nigga for looking at my bitch too long. This disrespect thing you got going on behind Heaven needs to get squashed today. It's bad for business! Every man at this table has a family and mouths to feed. Legacy Inc. is in a business deal with The St. Croix Cartel, but you already knew this. The bullshit ends today.

"I hear you loud and clear, Unc. Let me say this I'm not the one that hit you up and I've been telling you this for the longest. My issue is Heaven forgetting that I'm Remy Ma's daddy. I only showed up to that whack ass wedding today to see my fucking daughter. She can't keep my daughter from me and move her to another city without my permission. I wasn't the one that hit you up, but for Reminisce, I'll go to war behind her. As far as Heaven goes, I'm the first that felt that pussy. You ain't felt shit she ain't introduced me to. Heaven will always be my bitch!" I rubbed my hands together like Birdman listening to this fuck nigga.

"Let's get something straight. I'm not about to sit here and have a contest with you about my wife and my pussy. Remy Ma is your daughter, and she's my stepdaughter. She's the only reason I haven't moved on your ass. I've killed niggas for less, but the disrespect gone get you murked. You're still young minded, so you're walking around this bitch with a point to prove. That's not my style. The money is the motive, and that's all I'm interested in. You can sit here in front of your crew and front all you want. My nigga, you're sick that Heaven married me. If I were in your shoes, I would be sick too. You see, I know the quality she possesses. What was flawed in your eyesight shines bright like a diamond in my eyes. As far as her being your bitch, you'll never get your bitch back!

You sit at this table and speak so highly of your daughter, yet you hurt her mother at every turn. That's my wife, and wherever I go, she goes, which means the kids go to. I've never tried to step on your toes in regards to you being her father. However, I'll never sit back and allow you to play with my wife on no level. We can have a sit-down about visitation, but we're definitely moving to Atlanta. Feel free to visit anytime. Today is the last day we're discussing my wife."

"You got it, Cross the Boss!" he said sarcastically, which was cool with me as long as his bitch ass took heed to what I said.

"With that out of the way, let's talk about who the fuck could that have been shooting at us today," Priest voiced.

"We don't have any beefs. It's literally been a peace treaty out here in the Chi. I hate to break it to you, but this is definitely a beef y'all got. This has been a long ass day for all of us. All of our phones keep going off. It doesn't take a rocket scientist to know that's the wives calling. This is for you, Cross. Make sure you holla at me before you leave. Good looking out Priest and Saint, I like how you niggas move." Thug dapped it up with everyone, and we all disbursed.

I wasn't sure if the nigga Lil Dro got the picture. For his sake, I hope he did.

Riding back to the hotel. I looked at the documents Thug had given me. They were time-stamped videos of Lil Dro in Cali. He was telling the truth about not hitting me up. The other thing that caught my eye amazed me.

"Look at this shit!" I hit my hand on the steering wheel over and over again. A red camera light had caught a glimpse of the person who hit me at the intersection.

"Nah man! What the fuck?" Priest spoke as he ran his hand over his face in frustration

"That's Ghana!" Saint yelled!

"Exactly! If Ghana was the one that hit me up, that means Prentiss was behind the shit."

That shit hurt my heart. I don't even know what I did to this nigga, but I had to get to the bottom of it. Ghana was one of my father's most trusted assassins. If he sent her, he wanted you dead. If you lived after she got at you, then you were a lucky motherfucker.

"We need to get to Atlanta immediately. Him being behind the shooting and this shit that popped off today got me feeling like he's behind all of this shit!"

"Man Priest, what the fuck is this nigga on with us?" I had to ask even though I knew he was just as confused as I was.

"Listen. Let's just get home and deal with this shit. Let's keep this under wraps. Don't tell ma or Monae. Keep this shit under wraps with Heaven, Rasheeda, and especially Ketura. Y'all know my wife can't hold hot water."

I didn't respond to Saint I just sat in the damn driver's seat in deep thought about this shit. If you can't trust the nigga whose loins you come from, then who in the fuck can you trust. I was over this day. Heaven and I should have eloped. I know my baby is devastated and she deserves a damn do-over.

Walking into our suite, I was surprised to see Heaven sitting up breastfeeding our son, Cross St. Croix Jr. Every time I speak my son's name loudly, I get goosebumps. My lil nigga is going to be so powerful when he gets older. Heaven was so overprotective of him. All night since we had him a month ago, she wakes up to make sure he's breathing. The death of her son has her scarred mentally. Sometimes I have to just wrap my arms around her and reassure her that he's going to be okay.

"Where's Remy Ma?"

"My momma took her home with her until we leave Sunday. She wants to spend as much time with her before we officially move," she spoke somberly.

"I told you that you don't have to leave if you don't want to. I'll stay here if it makes you comfortable."

"Absolutely not. Atlanta is a plane ride away. If I get homesick, I can fly out there and see my family. My place is with you, and if that's Atlanta, then that is where I will be. A woman's place is with her husband. Plus, I've been through a lot in Chicago. It's time for a change of scenery. This will be better for all of us. Stop worrying about this move so much. As long as I have you, I know that I'll be okay. Go take a shower, babe. You look exhausted. I'm going to burp him and put him to sleep."

"Exhausted ain't the word." I hated to wear a worried expression on my face in front of her but knowing my father was behind the hit stirred my spirit.

"I usually never ask about your street business, but I need to know how the meeting went."

"Let's just say Lil Dro wasn't the trigger man in my shooting. Right now, our beef is on the back burner. Let's hope it stays that way. Hopefully, he'll step the fuck up and do right by that beautiful ass little girl he has. You know I love you, Remy Ma, and my son with all my heart. No matter what happens in this life, I'll always make sure y'all good. Don't worry about who shot me. That's my job. All I want you to do is be a mother to my kids and the best wife you can be. It's a lot of things I'm not sure of in this life, but you are the one thing I'm absolutely sure of. Thank you so much for making me the happiest nigga in the world." I kissed Heaven on the forehead and did the same to my son before heading to take a much-needed shower.

As I showered, I didn't know how much longer my brothers wanted me to wait before getting at our mother or our father. I would stand down for now until we came up with a for sure plan on how to proceed.

CHAPTER TWO
HEAVEN

HAD I known my wedding day would have been so fucked up, I would have eloped. Although I was bussing my gun right with Cross, it was traumatizing to watch people actually trying to kill him a second time. Cross is like the sweetest person in the world. I know that he's a kingpin and what the government may call a damn criminal, but at the same time, he moves so smoothly. He's the most humble nigga you want to meet. Most niggas with money as long as his would go out of their way to flaunt that shit, but not Cross. I've watched this man get out of the car and give every homeless person he sees one hundred dollars. Because I know that man's heart, I take it personally that people are trying to hurt him.

It felt so good to kill a couple of them motherfuckers. I was thanking my lucky stars that I was taught how to handle guns at an early age. Growing up with my momma and aunts, I learned how to lay a nigga down with precision, which was something I've always kept to myself. I'm positive Cross and my family were shocked as fuck seeing me get off today. I said I would hold my nigga down to the fullest, and I meant every fucking word.

After burping my son and placing him in the portable baby bed, I undressed and went to join Cross in the shower. The look on his face when he came inside of the suite let me know some shit kicked off at that meeting. Yah-Yah hadn't called me with no shit yet, so I guess shit was all good like Cross said.

Stepping inside of the shower, I kissed Cross on his back. He was leaning forward on the wall allowing the water to fall over his body. My baby was stressed the fuck out. Getting on my tippy toes, I placed a kiss on his neck and cheek. Cross turned around and wrapped his arms around me. I melted into his strong embrace. There was something about the way he hugged me and touched me. His touch was like a paintbrush that painted a pretty picture, and I was his canvas.

I took control as I pushed him up against the wall. Without hesitation, I dropped to my knees and started to murder the dick. I deep throated the dick as I massaged his balls. I flicked my tongue back and forth across his fat mushroom head, making sure to make those sucking and slurping sounds that drive him crazy. I knew that he was nearing is peak when he grabbed the back of my head. He started fucking the shit out of my face, and not long after, he was spilling his seeds down my throat.

Cross wasted no time pulling me up to my feet. He gently lifted me, and I wrapped my legs around his waist. This is absolutely my favorite position that Cross fucks me in. Something drives me crazy about the way he bounces me up and down on his dick. I can feel that nigga in my soul.

I was feeling pleasure and pain at the same time. This was my first time having sex since the birth of my son. It was a good thing I had been taking my birth control faithfully. Cross was fucking me so good that I would definitely be pregnant at my six-week check-up otherwise. For the next ten minutes, we fucked all over the shower, and until we were exhausted.

No sooner than our heads hit the pillow, Cross was out like a light. Listening to him snore lightly was soothing. I was happy that he could get some sleep. Lord knows sleep wasn't coming easy to me at the moment. Getting out of bed, I stared out of the huge window that overlooked the Chicago skyline. It was fucking beautiful at nighttime.

I still couldn't believe I was actually leaving it all to start a new life in Atlanta.

"You okay, babe?" Looking behind me, Cross was now sitting up in bed.

"Yeah, I'm okay." I walked back over to the bed and snuggling under him.

The sound of his strong heartbeat was so soothing to me. My mind was in full-blown overthinking mode. On the one hand, I was happy, and on the other hand, I was worried. I had everything I had wished for in the form of my husband and kids. However, I couldn't help but feel like there was something or someone in the shadows that was out to hurt us. Only time would tell. In the meantime, I was going to love and nurture my family like a wife is supposed to. It's best I put the worrying in the back of my mind. Its obvious Cross needs me to have a clear head and a shoulder to lean on while he tries to murder those that trespass against us. Goodbye, Chicago, hello Atlanta— I'm officially married to The St. Croix Cartel.

A Month Later

It had been a month since we officially moved to Atlanta. Life had been good so far. I would be lying if I said I wasn't homesick. The only thing that was keeping my mind off it was performing my wifely duties and tending to the kids. Cross had been gone a lot, and the only time we would really see each other was late at night when he made it home. For some reason, I could never sleep until he came in. No matter if the sun were coming up, I would sit up and wait. My son was on my schedule, so he slept when I slept. After waiting up for Cross all night, I would be exhausted during the morning. At first, I was dead set against having a nanny, but Cross felt like we needed one. After a big debate, I gave in and let him bring on Ms. Bam who was his nanny as a kid. She's also married to Bentley. Both of them have been a godsend with my transition from Chicago to Atlanta.

Since Cross had us living on this huge ass estate, we moved

Bentley and Ms. Bam inside of the guest house. At first, I didn't really care for the idea of having people living on the property, but they have both proven to be trustworthy in my eyes. I am finally comfortable with leaving the kids alone with Ms. Bam. I'm so overprotective of my kids, especially my son. I've been feeling like I need to talk to someone about my fear of him dying. The anxiety of it all consumes me daily. Lately, my deceased son has been on my mind heavily. I've been feeling guilty about being responsible for him passing away. I know it's God's will. At the same time, it doesn't make me feel any better. The only thing that strengthens me is wearing the necklace with his ashes in it daily. My baby boy is with me everywhere that I go.

"Please don't make me fall, babe." Cross had me blindfolded, and I was tripping all over the place.

"I'm not going to make you fall. Take one big step, and then I'm going to remove the blindfold."

I was so nervous trying to see what the hell Cross was up to. He removed the blindfold, and I almost lost my mind."

"Oh my god! This is so beautiful. Why didn't you tell me? I've been out looking for spaces."

The interior was beautiful with bright lights and sparkling chandeliers. The black and white painted walls gave it that girly look that I love. All of the stations were set up and ready for customers to come in.

"I wanted to surprise you. When you told me that you wanted a nail bar here, I hopped right on it. All I did was go with the same blueprint that Ace had for the first store. I know you love hot pink and black, not to mention sparkly shit, so that's the theme. Look at the chandeliers. They're the same ones you picked out for the house."

"Thank you so much." I wrapped my arms around Cross' neck and hugged him so tight. This man never ceases to amaze me. I've literally been breaking my neck to secure a place in Buckhead when he had shit covered all along.

"Why are you crying? I didn't do this to make you sad. I actually did this shit to make you happy. You uprooted yourself for me and left your businesses in someone else's hands out there. The least I could do was have some shit in place for you here. Wipe your face and let's go celebrate."

Cross wiped my tears and kissed me passionately. It was so damn luxurious.

"That's just it. I'm not crying because I'm sad. I'm crying because I'm extremely happy. You love me in ways I never thought possible. I love you so much!"

"I love you too. Your happiness is the most important thing to me. I don't give a fuck what is going on in my street life. You and the kids come first. Now come on, let's go get drinks at this hookah spot that I own."

"You're just a regular businessman, huh?" This was my first time hearing about him owning a hookah bar.

"I'm a jack of all trades, ma. Once I get the downtime, we need to go and see my lawyer. I need for you to get know him and sign some documents. With us being married, I want you to have access to everything that I own. It's essential that I update my will as well. Anything could happen, and I want you to be taking care of for the rest of your life."

"I'm already set for life, Cross. I don't need all of those things. As long as I have you, I'll be just fine. The last thing I want to do is talk about your will."

I grabbed his hand and basically pulled him out of the space. That shit he was talking about was going to put a damper on my spirit. This was the last thing I wanted to be discussing. We just got married, and he was talking about a damn will.

"I don't want to talk about it either, but it's very important. Come on. Let's head over to my spot."

Cross grabbed my hand, and we walked out of the shop. As we

got into the car to drive away, I couldn't wait to open the doors and get the business growing. I pray this shop does just as good as my shops in Chicago.

▭

As I sat and vibed to the music at the hookah lounge, I couldn't help but notice how everyone basically stopped whatever they were doing to greet Cross. If I didn't know him, I would think he was a celebrity. This was my first time being in this type of setting with him, and it was pretty cool. Cross had this spot looking like a man cave. Besides being able to smoke hookah, unlimited weed was at your disposal. I don't know what it was with him and having naked bitches parading around his business. Just like the car wash, this place had damn near naked bitches walking around serving the guys.

Watching Cross work the room, I can truly see why he gets that "boss" treatment when he walks into an establishment. My baby is a boss in his own right. When he walks into a room, he makes people part like the Red Sea, giving him space. He had my pussy real wet. This hookah and strawberry Hennessy had me ready for whatever.

"Are You Gonna Love Me" by Teyana Taylor came on, and I started to vibe in my seat. Looking across the room at Cross, he winked his eye at me. He knows this was my favorite song.

"Damn, beautiful! What you doing over here all alone?"

"I'm not alone. My husband is right there." I pointed at Cross, and the guy looked over at him. Cross had his shirt raised showing his chromed out Desert Eagle.

The nigga had his hands up to let him know he didn't want any trouble. From a distance, I watched as the guy walked over to Cross. He grabbed him by the back of his neck and said some shit in his ear. Seconds later, the guy was walking back over to me looking like he was about to cry.

"I'm sorry for disrespecting you, Mrs. St. Croix."

"It's okay." This man looked so pitiful, and I felt sorry for him. Cross had probably threatened to murder the poor man.

As he walked away, I smelled shit. Cross had scared this man so bad that he shitted on himself. I was embarrassed for him. The nigga walked out of the lounge, and three men in all black followed him out. I didn't even want to think about what they were going to do to him. I mean the one thing I'm not about to do is to sit and act slow. Cross was showing me firsthand he was a sweetheart that was ruthless as fuck. He didn't blink too hard or move from the spot he had been standing in the entire time. Cross went back to conversing with the crew of niggas he was talking with before.

As I sipped my drink and smoked the Hookah, I observed Cross. The guys were standing around quiet listening to him speak. It was as if they were hanging on to his every word. The entire lounge had been cool and laid back. Then a group of loud ass bitches entered the place and fucked up the vibe.

"Here you go, Mrs. St. Croix." The waitress came over and placed some hot wings and another strawberry Hennessy in front of me.

"I didn't order this."

"I know you didn't. Mr. St. Croix ordered it. By the way, I'm Kimmie, the manager. Anything you want or need just let me know."

"Thank you. It's nice to meet you." She extended her hand, and we shook hands with one another.

I'm glad I didn't get a bad vibe from her. Bitches always want to fuck their bosses, especially when he's rich and fine as fuck like Cross. Women just know. We can feel when a woman wants our man. This woman didn't come off like that. It didn't mean that I wouldn't be watching her ass though.

As I continued to sip on my drink, the urge to pee came on full force. My ass was tipsy as hell. My ass had to rush to get to the bathroom because if I didn't, it was going to be a pissy ass situation. Once I made it to the bathroom, I rushed inside of the stall. Moments later, I heard women come into the bathroom talking shit.

"I still can't believe the nigga went to Chicago got married and had a damn baby. That shit got me hot as fuck. Now he's in this bitch acting like months ago he wasn't at the hotel fucking my brains out. Did you see how he walked past me like he didn't know me?"

"Let that shit go, Ari! Cross has never wanted you like that. I told you a long time ago that nigga was out of your league. I heard the bitch he married got paper of her own. Your child support, food stamp, medical card having ass didn't stand a chance. I'm your blood sister, so I'm keeping it real with you."

"You tried it, hoe. I just wonder what she did to get him to notice her. I'm sure she pursued the fuck out of him. That nigga Cross don't chase bitches."

I couldn't take it anymore hearing her say that shit. Flushing the toilet, I walked out of the bathroom and looked at both of them. They looked like deer in headlights. Looking at them, I knew they weren't even worth me addressing. These bitches weren't even in my tax bracket. No words were needed. Being Mrs. St. Croix had the bitch pressed as hell. I'm secure in my position as Cross' wife, so I don't even have to address certain shit. I dried my hands and walked out of the bathroom as if I never heard anything they said. When I made it back to the section, Cross was sitting smoking on a blunt with Priest and Saint. Rasheeda and Ketura were there as well.

"You okay, babe?"

"Yes, Cross, I'm just fine. Hey everybody."

"What's good, sis?" Priest and Saint said at the same time. We exchanged hugs, and I joined them in the section.

"Look at you looking all pretty. It doesn't even look like you just had a baby," Ketura said followed by Rasheeda smacking me on the ass.

"I know, right. Heaven, you thicker than a Snicker." As we all laughed, I observed the girls that were in the bathroom coming towards the section.

"What's good, Cross?"

"Ain't shit good? Keep it moving." The words slipped from my mouth before I realized what I was doing.

I had let the bitch slide in the bathroom, but the blatant disrespect was not about to be ignored. This bitch was trying me right now. After the shit with Shieka and Lil Dro, I refused to allow a hoe to think she could play with me when it comes down to my nigga.

"Girl bye! You doing too much!"

"That's your problem. You didn't do enough. Beat your feet before you get beat the fuck up in here!"

"Really, Cross? This what you married."

"You heard my wife. Beat your feet bitch before I let her fuck you up!" I didn't expect for Cross to say that, but having my back was everything right now. The hoe finally walked off, looking embarrassed and feeling foolish as fuck.

"I like her, bro! She's going to fit into this family just fine. You with the shit, huh, Heaven?" Saint asked.

"She has to be! These hoes will try you at every turn. Speaking of hoes, yours just walked in! I advise you to keep the hoe on a leash, or I'm sliding her ass," Ketura spoke as she sipped from her drink. The conversation went left quick as hell.

"Calm the fuck down! If you're going to be in here acting a fool, you can take your ass home."

"Nigga, you want me to leave anyway so that you can be with that hoe. I'm not stupid, Saint."

"Bring your ass here! Let me holla at you." Saint stood to his feet and basically snatched Ketura out of the booth.

"Not here, bro. Y'all go home and handle that shit. We're about to get out of here anyway." Cross stood up and handed me my purse that was on the seat.

"We just got here, bro. Chill for a little while. The night is still young. Plus, I need to talk to you about some shit in private," Priest said, knocking back a shot.

"You good, babe?"

"Of course, go ahead. Rasheeda is here, so I'll be fine. Take your time."

"Okay cool. Don't be teaching my wife any of your bad habits, Sheeda."

"Boy bye!" You better believe she's about to get the rundown on being married to a damn St. Croix."

We all laughed as Priest and Cross left out of the section. In the distance, I observed Saint engaged in a conversation with a chick. I assumed that was who Ketura was referring to.

"Come outside with me. Ketura just texted me. I swear to God it's always some bullshit. I'm happy that you're married to Cross. I can tell he really loves you and you love him too. Make sure you always handle yourself exactly like you did today. I watched you kill some motherfuckers, so I know you can handle yourself in any situation. Trust me. There will always be a situation where you have to prove yourself to Cross and these people in the streets. It's sad but true."

Rasheeda drank the rest of her drink, and we both headed outside to check on Ketura. The last thing on my mind was anticipating the bad things that are sure to come. I'm a newlywed, and I prefer just to relish in the amazing feeling of being Cross St. Croix's wife. I'll deal with the bullshit when the time arises. It ain't shit Molly, my Mac-10, can't handle. I've come a long way from being weak ass Heaven. These bitches in Atlanta are not ready for the smoke I'm willing to bring behind Cross.

CHAPTER THREE
KETURA ST. CROIX

AS I SAT in my car in the parking lot of the hookah lounge, I was pissed. Saint had me feeling some type of way behind this bitch Shayla. It's like ever since this hoe popped up talking about she had a daughter by Saint, she's everywhere I am. She's walking around like she's entitled to some shit. This man is my whole husband and has been my husband for the last three years, not to mention we've been together for five.

I've been with Saint since I was twenty years old. I've been through hell and back with his ass. I've held him down with this street shit. It's not easy loving a nigga who is part of a fucking cartel, but I've done that shit with ease. I'm not a trophy wife that's sitting at home playing blind to my husband's whorish ass ways. I've known Saint fucks around, but that shit never graced our doorstep, and bitches knew to stay in the side bitch corner where they belonged, except this hoe Shayla. Her behavior makes me feel like he still fucking her. He has been going out of his way to prove to me he doesn't fuck with her, and it's strictly about their daughter. However, my woman's intuition is speaking loud and clear to me. She's never been wrong.

I accepted the fact he had a baby on me because I simply can't hold a baby. After years of trying with no luck, we both decided to stop trying to conceive. I was just never informed that he would be out trying with other people. Every day I walk around trying to act like everything is okay, but deep down inside, I'm hurting. Every time he walks in the door with that little girl, I cringe, and I feel hatred. I know it's wrong, but I can't help it. I would never hurt a child, but her presence hurts me. I haven't been very truthful with Saint about my acceptance of him having a child. The truth is, I resent him for hurting me. That added with this hoe Layla playing with me has me feeling like I'm to go crazy and spazz out.

"You good, boo?" Rasheeda asked as both she and Heaven got inside of the car.

"Not really, but I will be." I flamed up the blunt that I was smoking, and we all passed it around.

"Who is that chick?" Heaven asked.

"That chick is the bitch that has an eight-month-old daughter with my husband." I didn't even mean to start crying but just speaking the words hurt me so damn much.

"I'm sorry I asked, Ketura."

"It's okay, Heaven, just seeing her crawls my blood. I want to murder him and her ass. Saint is pissing me off acting like it's nothing. He really thinks his apology is enough to fix this shit. Plus, I feel like they're still fucking around."

I reached into the glove compartment and grabbed some napkins to wipe my face.

"That bitch knows what she be doing too. I hate that hoe. Just say the word, and we can get on bullshit quick." Rasheeda was always ready to turn up. That's what I love about her.

Grabbing my phone to scroll on my IG, I instantly became pissed. Here this hoe was posting a picture of her and my husband. My blood pressure literally went up so high that it felt like my head was going to explode. The caption was so fucking messy.

He gave me what I wanted. I gave him what she couldn't!
#SiennaParents

#Bonded4Life

As bad as I wanted to go off, I decided not to do it in front of Rasheeda and Heaven.

"Thanks for coming to check on me. I'm about to head home though. I'm not in the mood to go back in there. Let's all go shopping this weekend."

"Okay cool."

"That's good because I need to talk to y'all about my nail bar that I'm opening up here. After shopping, we can all go out to dinner," Heaven said so excited.

Inwardly I smiled because I remember being that happy in the beginning of my marriage. There had been in a shift in the atmosphere that disrupted my marriage, and it hurt so badly.

"I'm down. I'll see y'all Saturday."

Both Heaven and Rasheeda got out of the car and headed back inside the lounge. I didn't have the heart to walk back in there after seeing that picture. I don't know if I was more hurt or embarrassed about the situation. As I drove home in tears, I realized it was both and too much for me to take on at the moment

About an hour later, I was pulling up to our estate. It was the most beautiful thing I ever had a hand in building. Living in this home was a world away from where I started. I was raised in a small two-bedroom apartment in the projects. The house was always filled with relatives needing a place to stay. My mother never turned anyone around. That was just how her heart was set up. We were just always filled to capacity, and I never really had my own room growing up. I just always vowed to give myself the best of everything if I was ever afforded the opportunity. Growing up all my life, I promised myself that I would never go back to the projects once I got out. All of that added with living in a house with a father who was sick in the head was enough to never make me look back.

Meeting Saint was everything, and it wasn't about the money or the title he held in the streets. I loved how he loved me. Saint gave me a better life, but it cost me my dignity. I've compromised myself as a woman for this luxurious lifestyle all of these years. I'd rather live in the projects struggling than in a mansion unhappy.

At that moment, I felt so alone. I couldn't call my older sister, Kyrah. She didn't approve of my relationship with Saint. She killed me with her holier than thou bullshit. Her ass tricked a white, rich man into marrying her nutty ass, and now she swears she's a Christian woman. This is the same bitch that used to be doing dicks on her way to school.

I needed to talk to someone who wouldn't judge me for loving Saint, but instead give me wisdom on how to move forward with the situation. It had been a minute since I visited Mrs. St. Croix. She always gave the best advice. I loved that she was a woman first and a mother second. Jamaica had been the best mother-in-law a girl could ever ask for. I had the urge to do something crazy, and if I went home, that's exactly what would happen. Right now, I needed a voice of reason from someone who loved both of us. Then again, she had her own troubles. She had a husband in jail who wants to kill her, and she's been fucking his best friend for years. Plus she's still healing from Saint's father almost beating her to death. I needed just to take my ass home and deal with this nigga accordingly.

Driving back home, I had it all planned of what I wanted to say to him. The moment I walked inside the house, I forgot everything I wanted to say. He was asleep on the couch with his daughter asleep on his chest. At this point, I was too tired and emotionally drained to deal with it. No matter if I spoke on how I felt, nothing would change the fact he had a daughter on me, and I'm almost positive it was driving me crazy.

━━━

The next morning I woke up to find Saint gone and his daughter Sienna asleep in the bed next to me. This man had lost his mind because he hadn't even woke me up and asked me to keep her. In that moment, I had to show both him and his bitch ass baby momma to stop fucking with me. Jumping out of bed, I handled my personal hygiene and threw on a T-shirt with a pair of leggings. After placing on my gym shoes, I grabbed Sienna and headed out of the house. Saint was going to learn to stop playing with me.

Thirty minutes later, I pulled up to Shayla's apartment building. Of course, she and her slow ass friends were sitting out front drinking and smoking. I'll never understand how Saint slipped up and got this buzzard ass hoe pregnant. I had no words for her ass as I grabbed the car seat with Sienna in it from the backseat. I placed her daughter right on the ground in front of her.

"What are you doing bringing her here, Molly the Maid? Don't you know this your weekend? I have shit to do so I advise you to take her back home before I call Saint on your ass."

"I advise you and him to stop fucking playing with me. Now, I understand y'all have a child together, but I want no parts in the shit. You can call Saint and tell him whatever the fuck you choose to. He'll know next time before he leaves his fucking daughter at my house without my permission."

"Bitch, you're sad as fuck being jealous of an innocent little girl. Don't get mad at me because I gave your husband something you can't give him. I don't care what type of bullshit you try to pull. Nothing will change the fact that Sienna St. Croix exists. If we keep fucking the way we do, I might just give him a son. Saint St. Croix Jr. has a beautiful ass ring to it."

I could hear her and her whack ass crew laughing as I walked back to my car. I was not about to openly argue with this Section 8 having ass bitch. My ass had already lowered my standards by even pulling up. At the same time, I refused to keep getting disrespected by Saint and her. Instead of going back to the house, I headed to St. Croix Enterprises to holla at Saint. My phone was on the passenger seat going off like crazy, and I know it was him. If he wanted a fight in regards to this shit, I was definitely ready for whatever. It was a surprise that I wasn't pulled over by the police. My ass was doing way past the speed limit trying to get to Saint's ass.

Walking inside of St. Croix Enterprises, I headed straight to Saint's office. I bussed inside his office, and he was sitting behind his desk smoking a blunt. Why the fuck did he have to look so fucking good? From the wicks on the top of his head to the designer shoes he rocked on his feet, this man was perfection. Saint was tall in stature, light-skinned, with gold fronts. His juicy pink lips alone were enough to make any bitch fall in love. The moment I saw him lick his lips while we exchanged numbers, I knew I was going to marry his ass. Saint had the type of game that would talk a bitch right up out her panties, and that's exactly what the fuck happened with us. He took my ass out and fucked the shit out of me at the damn restaurant. I prayed he didn't try to fuck me now. That's what he does when he knows I'm mad. Saint knows I'm weak when it comes to his dick, but not this time. I'm standing firm and keeping my fucking legs closed.

"Do I look like a motherfucking baby sitter, nigga?" He sat blowing weed smoke in the air like I wasn't standing there. Feeling ignored, I knocked everything off of his desk.

"No, you don't look like a babysitter, but I'm going to need you to calm down!"

"Fuck calming down! I know that hoe called you and said I dropped that ugly ass baby off to her ass."

Before I could finish, he jumped from his desk and stared me down with murder in his eyes. I took some steps back to create some much-needed space between us. Saint has never put his hands on me, but he didn't have to. He was so powerful that his stern words and intimidating presence were enough to make me pips the fuck down.

"I understand you mad at me but don't ever call my daughter out of her name again. She's innocent, and it's not her fault that I hurt you. Today I had to make a quick run that was last minute, which required me to leave her at the house. The both of you were sleeping, and I didn't want to disturb either of y'all sleep. Had I known you would go off and take her back home, I would have taken my daughter to my mother's house. I apologize if you felt disrespected. At the same time, you know that this type of behavior will not get you shit but a negative ass response from me. I really want to lay hands on your ass, but you know that ain't me. Whatever you have on your chest you need to get it off.

Talk to me, Ke-Baby! If you don't tell me what's going on with you, I can't fix it, babe. You just called a little girl ugly, and I know your heart is not set up like that. If you can't accept her, then I'll make arrangements to see her outside of our home. I've hurt you, and if this is too much, I understand. However, the fact remains that Sienna is here, and we know that she's mine. You're my wife, and I want you to build a bond with my daughter."

"Why are you acting like this shit is normal? News flash my nigga, it's not. You cheated on me with a lowlife ass hoe and had a baby on me. You're going to have to accept the fact that it's hard to deal with this shit! You and the hoe parade around and shit on me in front of the world. She put a fucking picture of you and her on IG! Plus, I know you still fucking her. We haven't fucked lately, and you're usually laying that pipe to me every chance you get. I mean if it's over Saint, let me know. I'll bow out gracefully. That way you and that bitch can live happily ever after. Let's keep it one hundred. We both know I can't have kids. What future do we have? I'll move all of my shit out of the house, and you will never hear from me again.

"Get the fuck out my office, Ketura! Your ass is talking crazy right now. You and I both know this thing we got is until the casket drops. Stop fucking playing with me. I'm willing to do whatever you want, but leaving is not an option. Shayla ain't shit but Sienna's mother. The hoe is definitely not wife material. I could've married any bitch I wanted, but I fell in love with your nutty ass. Just because I had a baby with someone else, don't mean shit. You're my wife, and nothing will change that."

"That's what you don't get, Saint. That shit means everything to me. Because I am your wife, it changes everything. We have everything, and the one thing we've been trying for you have it with someone else." I pushed his ass away from me and left out of his office. Niggas kill me acting like the shit they do is okay.

My ass headed back to the house we shared because I had some soul searching to do. I currently really needed to figure out if staying in this marriage was what I wanted to do. Pulling up to my house, I couldn't believe my fucking eyes. Sienna's car seat was sitting on the doorstep. This hoe Shayla had lost her fucking mind. Now, I was about to beat her ass. Hopping out of the car, I rushed over to the car seat to see Sienna chewing her fingers up. The poor thing was hungry as ever, and she looked like she had been crying her eyes out. I didn't even bother to try and take her back to her pathetic ass momma or call her dumb ass daddy. The woman inside of me that has compassion decided to just tend to the baby. As much I hated the whole situation, I couldn't even bring myself to stoop any lower than I had today.

Lifting her from the seat, she was soaking wet. I couldn't believe this lady had dropped her baby off alone like this. After cleaning her up and feeding her a bottle, she was fast asleep. There I was in the same spot I woke up in this morning. Had I known this little girl would end up right back in my damn house, I would have never dropped her off in the first place. I realized exactly what Saint could do to make this shit up to me the more I stared at her chubby cheeks.

CHAPTER FOUR
SAINT ST. CROIX

A NIGGA DIDN'T KNOW if he was coming or going. Between dealing with the betrayal of my father and trying to keep the peace in my marriage, I was losing my damn mind. My father was refusing our visits, and my mother was fucking Haitian Jack, a nigga who just so happened to be my father's best friend. I was ready to kill this bitch Ghana, but Priest had us holding off on the shit until he could get with our Pops. He was going to need luck because Prentiss was on bullshit. I was a phone all away from hitting my people up on the inside and sending the word to off his ass. The moment I realized that nigga was plotting against Cross, he became an enemy of mine. This shit is bigger than him being with Heaven. Cross was a threat to him, and I didn't understand why. For Prentiss to send Ghana to personally handle Cross meant that he was out for blood. I was at my wit's end with waiting. Priest needed to say the word so that we could send a clear fucking message that the new and improved St. Croix Cartel was not to be fucked with. The waiting game with Priest gave me a chance to get shit right on the home front.

I know I've fucked up with Ketura by getting Shayla pregnant. The shit was never my fucking intention. Ketura is walking around thinking that I fucked around with Shayla out of the blue and she got pregnant. The truth was I had been fucking with Shayla off and on for years. She was a bitch I knew who would always be around to let me take my frustration out on the pussy. Shayla took dick in every hole and was a nasty bitch. She loved bringing her friends into the bedroom. Her pussy was dependable and added with the fact that we used her as a mule were the main reasons I kept the bitch around. Once she got pregnant I stopped fucking with her on a business level. Shayla got pregnant on purpose. When I found out, I couldn't bring myself to make her get rid of it. Knowing my wife can't have kids made me want Shayla to have the baby even more. I know it sounds fucked up, but the idea was that's the truth. I feel fucked up for hurting Ketura because she's definitely a down ass bitch. I've never had to question her love or loyalty. She's been through some shit with a nigga, but this baby shit has her speaking on leaving nigga. To hear her say that shit angered the fuck out of me. I was not fucking joking when I said this shit was until the casket drops.

Before heading home to talk to Ketura, I needed to check in on my OG. She hasn't been herself lately since all of this shit transpired with my father. The nigga had beaten her within an inch of her life and was picked up by the police hours later. When the police pulled him over, they found bricks in his trunk. He was definitely set up because he would never be riding dirty like that. My father is a beast at this drug game. Riding with bricks in the trunk was a rookie ass mistake. Now he's sitting his ass in jail with no bond facing life in prison. His ass is lucky he's in jail because he would be a dead ass man for putting his hands on my mother. I didn't give a fuck if he is my father. None of the shit made sense to me. He laid hands on his wife and put on a hit on his son. Yet, he never went after Haitian Jack. That shit is hell of suspect to me, and I won't rest until I find out why.

<hr>

"What brings you over here, son? Where is Ketura? I've been calling her phone all day, and she hasn't answered. She didn't show up for our weekly lunch, and that's not like her.

"I just wanted to come over and check on you. Ketura doesn't feel too good, ma. She might have her phone on don't disturb. When I get home, I'll make sure to tell her to call you. How is your arm?"

"It's okay. They just took the cast off the day before yesterday."

My mother was still the prettiest woman I had ever seen. She made growing up extremely easy while my father made the shit hard. My mother was the epitome of a down ass bitch. She would take a bullet for my father and stand beside him shooting shit. OG was nice with her shit. Who in the fuck you think taught me how to shoot. My OG is the reason why I ride around with Helen everywhere I go.

"I'm fine."

"Are you sure about that? You haven't really spoken on the issue with pops."

"I don't speak on it because there is nothing to speak on. He's in jail, and now you and your brothers are in charge of the cartel. That's what I always wanted for my boys."

"It's not that easy, ma. Are you aware he tried to have Ghana kill Cross? She was the one behind the shooting." I knew I wasn't even supposed to be over here telling her this shit, but she was too damn nonchalant right now.

"I wasn't aware of that. I'll make sure to look into it. In the meantime, I need you to go home and tend to your marriage before you end up like your father. When will you niggas learn that side bitches are bad for business and detrimental to your fucking health? You see, I'm not surprised that Ghana would do that. She's been your father's side bitch for the longest. Over the years, he has kept that hoe away from me. I see she likes to touch things that don't belong to her. My kids are definitely off limits. You out of all the kids know I don't fucking play about y'all. Ain't no need to be worried about me I'm just fine."

I wanted to speak on Haitian Jack, but I had already said too much in regards to Ghana. My mother had this look in her eye that let me know she was going after Ghana. Priest and Cross were going to be so mad that I said something. There was a method to my madness though. I was looking at the person who set Prentiss up. It wasn't what she said that let me know her ass did it. It was what she didn't say. Jamaica was something else and not to be fucked with. After sitting with her a little while longer, I headed home to the crib.

From the moment Ketura had left the office, I had been calling her phone. The bitch Shayla hadn't called since she wanted to argue about Ketura dropping our daughter off. One would think the hoe would be mad because her daughter was dropped off. She was more concerned with not being able to go out and kick it. I hung up on the hoe because I could care less about her going out. I didn't want to hear none of that shit the bitch was talking about.

Walking into the house, I was surprised to see Ketura in the kitchen cooking dinner. My dick got hard looking at her caramel colored skin that always glowed. Her booty cheeks were basically falling out the bottom of the shorts she had on. The matching half shirt had her flat stomach on display. Just looking at her maneuver around the kitchen had me wanting to lay her across the table and eat the shit out of her pussy. I loved seeing my dick glide in and out of her pink pussy. Ketura knew she was a bad bitch, and she carried herself as such. Out of all the bullshit we've ever been through, this Shayla situation is the first time I ever saw her openly express her emotions. Ketura was a hard body, and it took a lot for her to even cry. So, seeing her emotional about the situation fucked me up.

Noticing a whole bottle of wine gone and a freshly opened one let me know she was tipsy. She had the music playing, so I knew her ass was lit. I decided not to even bother her and let her continue enjoying herself. Heading up the stairs, I was shocked to see Sienna in her nursery. Without hesitation, I went right back downstairs. Ketura was sitting on a bar stool at the island. She was sipping on the wine and smoking on a fat ass blunt. The long jet black weave had her looking like a ghetto Queen.

"How did Sienna get here?"

"When I came home, she was on the front porch all alone."

"You didn't think to call me and tell me that?"

"Hell no! I didn't have time to call you. Your daughter was soaking wet and hungry because her unfit ass mother basically abandoned her. What would have happened had I not came home when I did? Earlier today, you asked what you could do to make this shit up to me. Well, I want Shayla gone and I want to raise Sienna as my own. That's the only way I'll accept this shit. I never want to see Shayla again or hear her fucking voice." Taking the blunt from her, I took a pull off it and handed it back.

"You want the bitch dead then kill her. After this shit she pulled, she'll never get Sienna back anyway."

"Nah! You're taking all of the fun out this shit. I want you to put a bullet in her head like you dropped your seed off in her womb. It's that fucking simple."

Ketura was turning me on getting on her boss shit. She's always been down for whatever, but this shit here was on another level. I stepped closer to her and moved her shorts to the side to play with that pussy

"Last time I checked I was the head of this family." I gently played with her clit as I spoke.

"You are the head of this family, and I'm your advisor. Right now, I'm advising you to get rid of that bitch! That hoe cannot co-exist with me. Today was the last day I'm dealing with her fucking disrespect. When you married me, you told me that my wish was your command. " Ketura pulled me in close and kissed me seductively with each word she spoke.

"I got you, babe."

"You promise."

She removed her top and exposed her perky breasts. Her nipples were sitting up, looking like chocolate drops. I nigga had to grab them and suck on them for a minute.

"I promise. I'm going to get rid of that bitch."

Pushing her back on the island, she quickly removed her shorts. For a couple of seconds, I stood back watching her spread her pussy lips apart. She knows that shit did something to a nigga. Every time she dipped her fingers inside of her pussy, they came out soaked in her juices. Dropping my pants, I wasted no time whipping my dick out. I made sure to smack up against her pulsating that clit. Watching her bite down on her bottom lip, I knew she was ready for the dick. Without hesitation, I rammed my dick up in her as far as I could.

"Ahhhhhhh! Waitttttt, Saint!" she screamed out as she tried to push me back, but I needed to punish the pussy.

She was throwing out orders like I was a fuck nigga. My baby needed to be reminded who the king of this motherfucking castle. Clearly, she had forgotten. At the same time, I loved her bossing up on my ass. The shit only made me want to fuck the shit out of her ass and watch her closely going forward. Ketura was dead ass serious about me murking Shayla.

"Move your motherfucking hand and take this dick! You told me earlier I hadn't been laying dick! This is why you acting a fool around this motherfucker!"

"Ahhhh shit! I'm cumming, Saint!"

"Let that shit go, baby. I want to see that motherfucker erupt all over the place. You hear me, Ketura? Show me what that pussy do!"

I sped up the pace and started to go crazy in the pussy. She was squirting with each thrust. Her juices were running all own my balls and all over the damn floor.

"Babyyyyyyyyy! I can't take any more."

"Yes, you can. This is just the beginning. Take your ass to my man cave and assume the position."

On shaky legs, she jumped down off the counter and rushed to the man cave. Removing all of my clothes, I headed into the man cave behind her. Grabbing a bottle of D'usse from the bar, I drank from the bottle and flamed up a blunt. Ketura was in the doggy style position in the sex chair that sat in the middle of the floor. Walking in front of her, I took my dick and rubbed it across her juicy lips. Ketura looked me in my eyes as she started going crazy sucking a nigga's dick. I needed to grab on to the chair to keep from losing my balance.

Ketura was sucking my dick with a point to prove. If I wasn't going to agree to murking Shayla's ass before, I was definitely going to do it now.

Ketura knew what the fuck to do with her mouth to get me to agree with shit. How she sucked my balls and dick at the same time was still a mystery to me after all of these years. She would eat the dick up with no problem. My wife didn't have a gag reflex, so she definitely did a dick with no hesitation. Not being able to take anymore, I stopped her from sucking my dick and dropped the dick off in her balls deep. Not long after, we were coming at the same time. The D'usse, the weed, and the pussy had me letting off all my seeds up in here. After a couple of more rounds, Sienna had woke up. As I now laid in our bed, I couldn't help but fall in love with the sight before me. Sienna was sleeping wildly with her arm draped around Ketura.

"Why are you staring at me like that?"

"Besides you being beautiful as fuck, I love seeing her lying up under you. I always imagined how you would look holding our baby. The look fits you, and I love it. Earlier tonight, you requested that I get rid of Shayla. For you, I'll do anything. I need you understood there is no backing out of this shit. If you want to raise Sienna as your own, you have to be all in. You will be her mother for the rest of her life. If you're serious about that shit, tell me now."

"Earlier, I felt like I wanted the bitch dead. Now that I've thought about it, it wouldn't change the fact that Sienna is not my daughter. I don't have the right to take her mother from her. I love you, Saint, and the last thing I want to do is leave you. At the same time, this shit can't happen again. I don't even want to hear about another bitch. I'll do whatever I can to assist you with Sienna, but you better check that hoe Shayla. She got one more time to cross me, and I'm going to murk her ass. I'm Ketura St. Croix, and you better not forget that shit. You're supposed to be my king, but your crown is tilted."

I didn't even have a come back to what she was saying because she was right. At the same time, my phone was ringing. Looking at it. I quickly declined the call. It was Shayla, and we had nothing to talk about right now. I would holla at her ass tomorrow. Not wanted to fuck up the mood I powered my phone off and went to sleep next to my favorite ladies.

The following day I woke up and headed straight over to talk to Shayla. I purposely made sure to leave my daughter behind. She didn't need to see me lay hands on her unfit ass mother. Her leaving our daughter Sienna on our fucking doorstep was unacceptable. That's what the fuck I get for having a baby with the pussy ass hoe. I should have let her suck my dick and never called the bitch back.

Pulling to the bitch's house, I wasn't surprised to see her or her hoe ass friends sitting outside smoking. Shayla was too bad of a bitch to be around here acting like a buzzard ass hoe. The bitch definitely tricked me. That whole boss bitch act she put on was a façade. I believe this hoe be drinking forty ounces when ain't nobody looking. It's not even noon and these hoes were drinking cheap ass Vodka. The look in her eyes let me know she was surprised to see me. I've never done a pop up. I've always let her know when I was coming or had her meet me somewhere. The bitch that I was looking at was the real Shayla.

"What you doing over here, Saint?"

"Unless you want to get embarrassed in front of your people, I advise you to step inside the house. " Shayla stood up and walked inside the house. She knew not to even play with me because I've had to lay hands on her ass before.

"Saint I—"

"Shut the fuck up, pussy ass hoe! I'm talking, and you're doing all the listening. If you cut me off, I'm going to smack the shit out of you. I should put a bullet in your fucking head for leaving my daughter on a fucking doorstep. Why the fuck would you think that shit would be okay?"

"It's your weekend. Don't come over here getting mad at me. Your jealous ass wife started it, so I finished it!"

I had to pinch the bridge of my nose to calm down and keep from going to jail. This hoe had to be retarded or slow as fuck.

"Let's not even bring Ketura into this. The difference between you and Ketura is that Sienna is your fucking daughter, not hers. She might not be one hundred percent with accepting the fact we have a daughter together, but at least she had the decency to bring Sienna to you, unlike your stupid ass. You know what the fuck I do and what's going on. What if you a nigga had snatched her up and held her for ransom?"

"But she wasn't snatched up. I knew that shit wasn't going to happen. Ain't nobody crazy to pull that type of stunt with you or your family. That's why I was comfortable with doing it. Ketura had no fucking business bringing Sienna home anyway. My daughter is none of her concern. That bitch is just jealous of my daughter with her evil hearted ass! I'll be glad when you leave that hoe so that we can be a family!" I didn't mean to laugh, but this hoe had lost her mind.

"I would never leave my wife for your ghetto, forty-ounce drinking, bottom of the barrel, cum guzzling, dick sucking, trap house living, dirty feet having ass. As a matter of fact hoe, you tricked me acting like you was a boss bitch. Who clothes your ass be having on when you come around me? I'm looking at you right now Shayla, and I'm almost positive you smoke crack! That shit is a cause for fucking concern! Look at this fucking house. This that shit that be on them damn TV shows about them nasty ass people who don't clean up for years. Wait a minute. Is that a mouse on the mousetrap? Pussy ass hoe, you got my daughter living in this fucking filth! Show me her room that I gave you the money to put together."

Now she was crying because I was almost positive this hoe had played me. She wasn't moving, so I grabbed her by the ugly as wig she had on.

"Stop it, Saint!"

"Shut the fuck up!"

I pulled her by the hair through the entire house. I was disgusted, to say the least. It was only a two-bedroom house, so there was no reason why it should look like this. The kitchen was so fucking filthy that it looked like it hadn't been clean up in months. I just realized the type of hoe that I was dealing with. She was of them pretty bitches with badass hygiene. To the world, she was a bad bitch, but behind closed doors, she was a filthy ass animal. I was literally sick to my stomach realizing that I had stuck my pretty ass dick into some shit like this!

"Please stop, Saint! I swear I'm going to clean it up. I still have the money in my account you gave me for Sienna's bedroom.

"Keep that shit and take some fucking housekeeping classes. My daughter will never step foot back in this nasty motherfucker! Consider your fucking parenting card revoked, nasty trifling ass bitch!" I pushed her ass away from me so hard that I made her ass fall into the wall.

"You can't take my baby away from me! I knew you were going to take my baby and give it to that bitch. I swear to God I'll kill you and that hoe!"

I was heading out of the house but quickly turned around hearing that hoe threaten me. I pulled my gun out and started shooting in her direction but made sure not to hit her. I just wanted to scare the fuck out her. I was successful cause the bitch had piss running down her fucking legs. I rushed her and placed my gun in the middle of her forehead.

"Don't ever in your life threaten me or my wife you pissy, pussy ass hoe! Shayla, I do not want to murder you, so I suggest you get your shit together before attempting to even see Sienna. Don't even think about stepping foot into any St. Croix owned establishments. You're not in the position to be out partying and drinking. You're an unfit filthy ass bitch, and I don't even want to see your face. Your presence makes me itch. Looking at you right now got me feeling like I need to get baptized in bleach, ammonia, and anything else that will cleanse me of your nasty trifling ass! Stay the fuck away from me before I put a bullet in your head!"

I walked out of her house, and there were two squad cars in the driveway.

"Is everything okay, Mr. St. Croix?" Officer Miller asked me. The police department is on our payroll, so I was good.

"Yes, Miller, I'm good. Thanks for asking." We shook hands, and I hopped in my Benz and peeled off.

This hoe had me so fucking mad that I needed a damn drink. I was so disgusted that I needed to get fucked up because this hoe had pulled a fast one on my ass. This shit had my ass hot. A nigga had the right mind to turn around and kill her ass. All I could think about was how my daughter had been living in that filth. I had to take my ass home and tell Ketura that Sienna had to stay with us. There was no way that I could let her go back there.

CHAPTER FIVE
PRIEST ST. CROIX

GOING through the month's books being pissed was an understatement. In a matter of sixty days, we had lost well over twenty million dollars. All of the money we had lost was lucrative investments with other cartels. With them all backing out, it didn't take a rocket scientist to figure out way. Prentiss was locked up, and these motherfuckers thought we couldn't handle this shit. I took that shit personal ass fuck. With Prentiss' bitch ass being gone, I was now running shit with my brothers. We've put in too much work to allow the nigga to fuck over our bread. Prentiss fucking days were numbered. It was bad enough his bitch ass had laid hands on my OG. I'm still pissed he got knocked before I could knock him the fuck out.

I still hadn't forgiven his ass for disrespecting Rasheeda. For him to turn around and try to kill my fucking brother has me hating his ass. I had been holding off on getting at that nigga strictly because of the family ties. However, family ties can be broken. He's supposed to be the head of the household, but he got in his feelings behind my OG and Haitian Jack. All my life the man taught me to keep shit gangsta no matter the situation. Now he's out here wearing his emotions on his sleeve like a bitch. I've been holding off on making a move, but the way these numbers looking, we have to make a fucking move now. The nigga had the new and improved St. Croix Cartel fucked up!

Being the oldest of my siblings, it's always been my job to take care of my siblings. I've always been the best big brother that I could be. Both of my parents taught me to always put myself last and have them come first. That's why I've always been the brains of the operation. I'm the one that solves the problem logically, Saint solves them with Helen, and Cross solves shit the boss way— with a handshake and a bullet to your head. As a unit, we solve shit the St. Croix way with that gunplay. We don't do too much talking.

This is the longest we've held off on making a move against someone. The shit truly hurts a gangsta like me to have to kill the man that helped bring me into this world. If we have to take the nigga out, then so be it. There can only be one head of the St. Croix Cartel, and Prentiss will never have that title again. Heavy is the head that wears the crown, and I'm rocking the shit out of it. His bitch might as well gracefully bow out and king me!

⬛▭

"You mean to tell me the Vargas, Marconi, and Villanueva families all pulled out of the gun deal?" Cross asked in a heated tone.

I knew that he would be pissed behind this shit. After all, he had secured the majority of the business deals with the other cartels. Cross was the youngest, and at twenty-five, he was very business savvy. One would think he went to college for the shit, but he didn't. It's like he had the gift of the gab.

"Hell yeah, nigga! Prentiss is stopping all the fucking deals he had us establish."

"We need to just go and have a sit down with this nigga. I'm tired of sitting around losing money behind this nigga. If we gone run this fucking family, we need to make some noise, and he needs to be the—"

"We can't, Saint! He's in protective custody and visits from us are not wanted. In order for us to get down to the bottom of this, I think we should go see Uncle Pope. Outside of Haitian Jack, he knows how Prentiss moves!" I flamed up a blunt and watched as both of my brothers were in deep thought.

"Fuck going to talk to Uncle Pope! We're going to talk that nigga Haitian Jack! If Prentiss wants to act like a bitch lets go to the source that got him in his feelings." Cross said as I handed the blunt to him.

"I agree we need to go and holla at his bitch ass!" Both Saint and Cross were both standing to their feet and ready to go see Haitian Jack. I really wasn't feeling it, but we needed to see what the fuck was going on.

"Fuck it! Let's go holla at the nigga."

"Where the fuck you going in that suit, bro? Damn Priest, must you always dress like you Shaft or some shit!" This nigga Saint really thinks he a fucking comedian. Cross doesn't make the shit any better by laughing like it's the funniest shit he's heard all day.

"In case you forgot, I'm at the motherfucking office! I'm a businessman, my nigga. I make billion-dollar business deals. Don't nobody want to do business with a nigga in street clothes. Both of you niggas know when I put my shit on all eyes be on me! Whether I'm rocking a suit and tie or Jordans and jeans, the bitches love me."

"The last bitch that loved you got murked! Don't fucking play with me, Priest St. Croix."

My wife Rasheeda had walked in on the last part of the conversation. The last thing I needed was to deal with her bullshit today. We had been beefing for the past week behind some bitch sitting in the nail shop describing my dick. I distinctly told my security not to let this nut in the building this morning. Rasheeda hasn't given a nigga a peaceful moment since she overheard the bitch talking shit.

"What the fuck do I pay security for? Why the hell you here, Rasheeda?"

"I'm here because you blocked me! What type of husband blocks their wife?"

"The type of husband that might have to murder your ass behind your fucking mouth. I blocked your dumb ass because you won't stop calling me with the bullshit. In case you don't realize it, this is my place of business. As you can see, my brothers and I are discussing business. Whatever you need to talk about can be discussed at home. This ghetto ass behavior is starting to get on my nerves. Take your ass home!"

"Fuck you, Priest!" You better hope my ghetto ass be there when you come home. "

"For the sake of your life, you better be there!" She stomped out of the office and slammed the door behind her.

"Man, Rasheeda be on good bullshit!" Saint said as he checked his phone

"That bitch crazy is what the fuck she is. We've been arguing about a week behind the incident at the nail shop. I don't even know who the fuck this bitch is. Rasheeda's ass is basically mad because the description of some nigga dick sounds like mines. She even took a picture of the bitch. I've never seen that hoe a day in my life!"

I had to rub my temples to try and soothe the headache that was sure to come. My ass hadn't cheated or been on bullshit for a minute. Rasheeda makes the shit so hard with her nagging and insecurities.

"Bro, Rasheeda's been crazy. I don't know how you niggas do it. Heaven and I are good on all that bullshit."

Cross spoke with so much confidence, which was cool. I loved that my little brother found someone who he is comfortable enough to give all of his love too. I'm happy that Heaven found a nigga that won't be on bullshit with her heart. They're both young and experiencing true love for the first time. Shit is always good in the beginning. The same strong love they have now has to be even stronger to stand the test of time. Love is the only thing that has made me keep from murking Rasheeda. That's my baby, but she's crazier than a fly on shit.

"Let's see will you be saying that shit five years from now! Now come on let's go holla at this nigga Haitian Jack!" Saint said as he stood to his feet.

Both Cross and I followed him out of the office. I needed to get this shit over with so that I could go home and give Rasheeda some dick. That's obviously what the fuck she needs.

━━━

"Leave the guns in the truck!"

"Nigga is you crazy! I don't go nowhere without Helen, and you know that!"

"Right! Fuck I look like leaving my shit in the truck! I'm not going around a bunch of crazy ass Haitians without my shit! Cross agreed with Saint, but neither of them never logically thought when it came to shit like this. Then again, Cross was right. This old ass nigga had the Zoes on lock.

"We're coming to this man place of business without being invited. Let's just keep this shit professional so that we can get the answers. I am not dressed for a gunfight."

"Nigga, please! Your ass is dressed like Shaft. Trust me. You ready for a gunfight."

"Fuck you, Saint!" We all laughed and got out of the car.

Heading up to Haitian Jack's office, we were immediately met by about twenty Zoe niggas with their guns out. We quickly aimed our shit at them without hesitation.

"We come in peace! You niggas need to put them guns away, and we will put ours away. Let Jack know we're here."

"Jack is busy at the moment, but I'll let him know you stopped by."

"Are you hard of hearing, my nigga? Let Jack know The St. Croix family is here to see him." Saint gritted with his teeth with Helen aimed and ready to fire. I think he wanted one of their ass to flinch so that he could find a reason to kill one these motherfuckers.

"I heard you loud and clear. Like I said, Jack is busy at the moment, and he's not taking any visitors." Before we could respond to the nigga, Haitian Jack himself stepped outside.

"Listen right now is not a good time. I'll come over to your head-quarters first thing tomorrow, and we can talk about whatever it is you like."

"We have all day, my nigga. We'll sit out here until the time is right," Cross spoke up with his gun still trained on his men.

"Because we came to your spot unannounced I'll respect the fact you're busy at the moment. I'll reach out later with the location. Tell your people to stand the fuck down and to never point a fucking gun at my brothers or me again. Let's get out of here." I stared at his ass intensely before walking back off to the truck.

"We should have moved on his ass! He was lying. His ass was not busy at all."

"That's why we not about to anywhere. Let's circle the block a couple of times."

It was a reason why the nigga couldn't talk. I couldn't necessarily be mad because we did pop up without reaching out first. After driving around a couple of times, we finally got the answer we thought we wanted.

"Ain't this about a bitch!" Cross yelled!

"I knew that nigga was on some bullshit." Saint grabbed Helen and jumped out of the truck before it came to a complete stop. Putting it in park, I jumped out as well with Cross right beside me.

"Give me one reason why I shouldn't murk this nigga?"

"What the fuck you doing here, ma? So, pops was right when he said you fucking this nigga?"

"Watch your mouth, Priest! Put that gun down Saint before I beat your ass with it! Stop threatening him, Cross!"

"You love this fuck nigga or some shit! In case you missed the fucking memo, our father tried to have me killed. He almost beat your ass within an inch of your life, and now I see why. This shit is wrong as fuck! He supposed to be pops best friend and you fucking the nigga. Fuck is wrong with y'all right now!" Cross was going crazy. I had to take his gun out his hand before he fucked around and shot our OG by mistake.

"What's the fuck is really going on, ma? This shit got us looking at you sideways. You're the cause of all this drama. Our business is in jeopardy because you fucking this man."

I hated to be disrespectful to my mother, but she was disrespecting herself as a woman, a wife, and a mother.

"I know how this may look, but please let me explain. Y'all know I love y'all more than anything in this world. I'll tell you all everything but not here though." She wiped the tears that had fallen down her face. Usually, I would feel sorry and want to comfort her, not now though. She was the key to all the bullshit that was going on around us.

"Don't cry J-Baby?" Haitian Jack said, and it burned me the fuck up. In that moment, I didn't see a nigga who loved my mother. I saw a nigga who wanted what my father had built.

"Her name is Jamaica St. Croix! Don't ever call her anything else but that! Fuck is wrong with you, nigga?" Saint gritted, and my mother quickly stood in front of him.

"Let me get the fuck out of here! At this point, I don't even give a fuck. This shit is getting more and more fucked up!

"Don't leave, Cross. Give your mother a chance to speak her truth. You never have to fuck with me, but at the end of the day, she's still your mother. I'll give y'all some privacy to talk. Y'all can go to the office at the end of the hall." He kissed my mother on the lips and walked away like it was nothing.

"I'm about to kill this nigga!" I had to hold Saint back because he literally wanted to kill this man.

"Fuck y'all looking at? Anybody can feel this heat!" Cross was walking up on Haitian Jack's men who were still standing guard. These niggas were like loose cannons. That's why I wanted them to leave their guns in the car.

"Stop this shit, okay! I understand that you're mad or whatever, but don't ever disrespect me like this again. Meet me at my house. I want to discuss this shit in the privacy of my home."

"It funny how you want privacy but just let that nigga kiss you in the open."

"Shut the fuck up Saint, or I swear to God I will kill you with my bare fucking hands."

"Go ahead, ma. We'll meet you over there." She quickly walked past us and to her car. On the drive, we were all quiet despite the sound of my phone continually going off with notifications of an email. I didn't have time to check it. Right now, I needed to get down to the bottom of all this drama.

⎯⎯

About an hour later, we were all sitting around the dining room table. It felt funny being in the house that we grew up in. Sitting here without my little sister Monae had me missing her spoiled ass. That nigga Lil Ace needed move down here. I hated her being out there in Chicago. My only consolation that he was a solid ass dude, and I knew that he was taking good care of her. My mother had D'usse, shot glasses, and blunts all laid out in front of us. If we needed a damn drink and weed to listen to this, then it had to be some bullshit. The tension in the room was thick, and I could tell my mother was hesitating to talk.

"So, how long has this thing with you and Haitian Jack been going on?"

"Honestly, I was in a relationship with him before Prentiss. He went to jail, and that's how I ended up with your father, I became pregnant with you Priest, and it was like I stayed pregnant. All of those years Jack and I would fuck around from time to time. It was nothing too heavy though. I tried to respect him and Prentiss' friendship and their business relationship, and he tried to be respectful of my marriage and you kids. The love we have for each other has always been there. It wasn't until recently that we started messing around with one another heavy.

About a year ago, I found out your father and Ghana have been having an affair. When I went to Turks and Caicos, I logged into our security system and saw them having sex in my home, in the bed that we shared. I never confronted him about anything with that woman because I knew one day I was going to get their asses back. I've always had to move smartly to ensure that you boys inherit this dynasty. After all the work you put in, you deserve this shit.

"I don't mean to cut you off ma, but how does any of this tie into Cross being hit up?"

I needed her to cut to the chase. I really didn't care about the affairs. My concerns were my brother being hit up and why the fuck Prentiss was fucking with our bread.

"Thanks for asking that. You see Ghana and Prentiss have a son together. I've never even known the bitch had kids. He has the nerve to be named Prentiss St. Croix Jr. He and Cross are the same age."

"Wait a minute! How do you know all of this, ma?"

"Haitian Jack, of course. You see this pussy right here got power! I can get that man to do anything I want. Don't ever think your mother is just some whore who is out here fucking to be fucking. I fuck for more than just pleasure. I've been fucking with a nigga for the sole purpose of having leverage over Prentiss so that he can no longer be the head of this family. You see the only reason Haitian Jack is fucking with me so heavy is because he thinks I'm so dick silly that I'm going to help him take over the family business. His day of reckoning is coming soon enough."

"So, Ghana has a son with pops. I'm still not understanding why this bitch hit me up!"

"If any of you are dead, then her child gets this shit! It was easier to get at you first. You were out in Chicago beefing with Heaven's baby daddy, and he was the perfect scapegoat. I'm almost positive that hoe is plotting as we speak.

"Do you think pops told her to do the shit?"

"No, Cross. Prentiss may be a low down motherfucker, but he loves his kids. That whole thing with him not wanting you to be fucking with Heaven was strictly him being protective. Apparently, the people she's kin to are supposed to be some stone cold killers. I met them folks, and they seemed nice, especially that fine one they call Thug. If I wasn't old enough to be his mother, he could get it. Never mind all that. Either way, Prentiss was wrong for the way he handled that situation. You all have the right to choose who the fuck you want to be with.

"We need to go holla at the bitch Ghana and her long lost son. They both have to be murked! The last thing we need is this type of fucking drama. This shit is already bad for business. "

"I've been looking all over for her, and she's MIA. Don't worry Saint, snakes love to come out and hiss. They can't stay hidden for too long . Plus, she's in love with Prentiss. On everything that I love and that is holy, I'm going to kill that bitch for shooting you, Cross. I know you boys want that hoe's head on a platter, but let momma handle it. This shit is personal."

My momma knocked back a shot and took a long pull from her Newport. It's been years since I saw this side of Jamaica St. Croix, and I loved it.

"Damn, ma! You back on your gangsta shit, huh?" I said as I flamed up a blunt.

"I've always been on my gangsta shit. I just decided to put being a mother to you kids ahead of the street shit. This shit that we discussed is not to leave this room. I definitely don't want Monae knowing anything about this. She's in Chicago away from all of this bullshit, and that's how I want it to stay."

"So, what's the plan? We just sit back and wait for this shit to play out. I'm not one hundred percent sure Prentiss is not against us. How do we know he's not in protective custody because he's a rat? For all we know, he could be ratting all of us out!"

"No, Cross. Prentiss is a lot of things, but a rat he would never be. He takes this St. Croix shit to heart. He'll spend the rest of his life in jail or die before he does some shit like that. I've been with that man since I was fifteen. I'm fifty- five now, and I've been through so much bullshit with your father. I don't give a fuck about the bad shit. I'll always make sure to speak on the good shit. That man is ten toes down for the St. Croix Cartel. I can assure you he's not in there bringing down everything that he has built. That's why y'all need to keep this going. Move them bricks. Reach out to the ones that have backed out of deals and handle that shit. We're The St. Croix Cartel, and we bar none! Let's get to the paper."

My OG was so serious about the shit she was speaking. Both of my brothers and I sat listening, taking in every word. A lot wasn't said afterwards. We all agreed with what she was saying. As the matriarch of the family, we had to let her think the ball was in her court. No matter what we still need to work behind the scenes and handle shit our way. I loved my mother, and her word is always bond. At the same time, it was a lot of disloyal and treacherous motherfuckers around us.

After leaving my mother's house, we all agreed to beef up security. Cross was going to go and negotiate with the families that had pulled out. Hopefully, we can reestablish ties and get shit popping. With having my mindset in a good place in regards to my family business, I needed to get home and find out what the fuck was wrong with Rasheeda.

On the way to the crib, I stopped by Pandora to grab her some charms for her bracelet. She's always talking about how she wants to write a book, but she starts and never finishes. I feel like if I get her some charms that represent her as an author, it might motivate her to start the book. I even took it a step further and went to the Apple store and copped her the rose gold MacBook she had been eyeing. We already had a home office built for her so now all she had to do was sit and get this shit started.

If she busies herself with things that make her happy, she won't be running around this motherfucker with the insecurities. She would be so busy that me fucking another bitch wouldn't cross her mind. Granted I've done some fucked up shit in regards to fucking other bitches. Her insecurity is definitely my fault. As a man, I can stand up in my truth and admit my fuck up. It's just that I've been on my best behavior because it's a bitch out here that can hold me down like my Sheeda Baby.

I've literally given her the best life a woman could ever ask for. I've never asked her to do anything but be a good wife and mother to our two kids, Priest Jr. and Caprice. The woman she has become today is different from the woman I met ten years ago. When I met Rasheeda, she was hustling dime bags out of the projects where she stayed with her people. She was one of the many female workers who worked for The St. Croix organization. I took one look at her beautiful ass and knew that she was going to be my wife. I've never seen a female so fucking gorgeous in my life. Usually, a bitch that hangs around a bunch of niggas is a turn-off. Rasheeda was different though. I would sit back and watch her from a distance. She was always about business. She didn't fuck off or act trashy around the niggas she got money with. After watching her for months, I finally stepped to her. That shit was a first for me because I never was the type of nigga that chose a bitch. I let a bitch do all the choosing. I've always been the type of nigga that bitches flocked too. I had no idea what it was about Rasheeda, but I knew I wanted her rocking my last name. A nigga wouldn't have the shit any other way.

As I headed to the crib, my phone was still going off with emails. I knew if I opened up and it was business, I would head to the office. Tonight I just wanted to make shit right with my wife. Rasheeda needs to know that I do appreciate her and love her for sticking it out with me. Even on the days when I really didn't deserve her.

"Hey, daddyyyy!" My four-year-old daughter, Caprice, ran and jumped into my arms. She was very much the spoiled princess her mother made her into. I wouldn't have it any other way. It's so dope having a son, but having a daughter is the best blessing for any man.

"Hey, daddy baby! I missed you. Where is your brother and momma?"

"PJ is in his room playing that stupid game, and momma is on the patio sipping her wine and listening to Mary J. Blige. What did you do now?" she asked with her hands on her hips. Her is spoiled and grown at the same damn time.

"I didn't do anything. Daddy has been on his best behavior!"

"Okay good. Did you buy me anything from Pandora? My bracelet needs a new charm."

"Of course, I got you something. It's not a charm though. It's another pair of earrings. Take them upstairs and put them in your jewelry box. I need to go out here and talk to mommy." I placed a kiss on her forehead and headed out to the patio to check on Rasheeda.

"What's good, ma?"

"Nothing, my ghetto ass is just chilling." Her voice was dripping with sarcasm.

"I'm sorry about calling you that earlier. At the same time, you know not to act like that. You barged into my office while I was discussing business with my brothers, what if that had been investors or some of my other clients? You were disrespectful today, Rasheeda."

"What was disrespectful was you putting your wife on the fucking block list? You be mad when I pop the fuck off Priest, but you be doing shit to provoke me!"

"Stop yelling and calm the fuck down. This is a civilized conversation. It doesn't call for you acting all crazy and shit. Learn to speak in a lady-like manner. After all of these years, you should know I'm not talking if you yelling. Now, what's the problem, Sheeda?"

"The problem is you still cheating on me. When is this shit going to stop? We've been together for ten years. We have two beautiful kids. For Christ Sake Priest, we have a great life. Am I not enough for you?"

Rasheeda was on the verge of tears, and that fucked me up. I grabbed her by the hand and pulled her in close to me.

"Let me tell you something, Rasheeda St. Croix. You're more than enough. I don't care what bitch I've fucked in the past during our relationship. Them hoes don't compare. Now, I don't know why you're hell-bent on saying that I'm cheating on you because I'm not. I swear to God baby a nigga's been faithful. Since that situation with Keela, I've been on my best behavior. The last thing I need is to have to bury another bitch you've put a bullet in. I'm sorry that bitch played mind games with you at that salon. I'm telling you the honest to God truth. I don't know that bitch. I'm lost as to why you're even questioning me about the shit. I've never been a liar when it came to other women. I've kept that shit one hundred with you. Rasheeda, you're my right hand in this shit. You're far too beautiful and sexy to ever be insecure. I got you something."

I handed her the bags, and her face lit up looking at the MacBook.

"I already have a perfectly fine computer. Why would you buy me this one?"

"Well, I remember you saying you wanted the rose gold one. Plus, I thought maybe if I got you a new one, it would motivate you to write the book that you've been wanting to write. You need something to occupy your time, baby. You're a great wife and a wonderful mother, but you need to find something that's special just for you.

"Thank you so much. I think you're right. I do need to go ahead and start writing. My office is filled with journals of storylines and plots. This is exactly what I need to busy myself. These charms are so pretty. In a minute, I'll need a new bracelet. This one is almost filled up. Thank you so much for thinking of me, baby. I apologize for my behavior. It's just that when that hoe was talking and describing the nigga's dick, it sounded just like yours. I know it sounds crazy. Every since I killed that bitch Keela, it's like my senses are heightened.

If your phone rings in the middle of the night, I immediately think it's a bitch. You have to understand that my insecurities in this marriage didn't pop up out of the blue. Your infidelity made me this way. I know my behavior might piss you off, but you have to understand, you made me this way. As your wife and the mother of your children, I always want to be secure in my marriage. If you think I want to always look at you with a questioning eye, you're wrong. I love you, Priest, and I promise to do better with my behavior. You just make sure you be on your best behavior."

We engaged in a passionate kiss right before we interrupted by someone clearing their throat."

"Umm, excuse me. I'm hungry. Can a sister get some nuggets from McDonald's or what?"

"Get your hand off your hips and stop twirling your neck at me. Caprice St. Croix, you are not grown. I've told you to stop talking to us like we're your friends."

Rasheeda kills me getting on her about her attitude, but she created the little monster.

"I'm sorry, ma dukes. Can I please have some nuggets? PJ is hungry too."

"I am not hungry."

"Really, bro? That's how you gone do me. I'll remember that when you want me to give that bald head girl in your classroom a note for you."

"Okay. That's enough. Go get in the car. Daddy will take you to McDonald's. I have a book to start on, ain't that right, baby?"

"Yeah! That's right. I'm proud of you, and I'm going to support you every step of the way."

We exchanged more kisses before Caprice interrupted us again.

"Get a room! I'll be in the car!" I couldn't help but laugh at her. I loved to come home to this vibe. My family is my safe place. They're my escape from the world of being a St. Croix. Don't get me wrong. I embrace that life because it's in my blood, but some days the shit becomes too much. Rasheeda and my kids make the shit easier to deal with. I've had my partying days, the days where it was a joy to fuck as many bitches as I could, and I enjoyed being a menace to society. Nowadays I just want to get this money and come home to my family. It's a lot of bullshit on the horizon in regards to the St. Croix Cartel, so I need shit to be good on the home front. Hopefully, we can keep this shit on the right track.

CHAPTER SIX
RASHEEDA ST. CROIX

MOST WOMEN WOULD LOOK at my life and swear it was everything. Honestly, in a sense, it really is everything. Being the wife of a St. Croix definitely has its perks. At the same time, those same perks come with plenty of pitfalls and heartaches. I won't sit and make it seem like being married to Priest St. Croix is the worst thing that ever happened to me. In all actuality, being married to him what saved my life. Before meeting him, my ass lived recklessly as fuck. I used to hang with nothing but hustlers and gangsters. I sold drugs right alongside them. That's how I met Priest. Shocked was an understatement when I found out I was actually working for his family.

The moment he came at me, he wanted to change who I was. Hanging with niggas was such a turn off for him. Priest couldn't understand why I didn't have any female friends. I've never been the female that hung with bitches. Females have and will always be messy. I'm one of those bitches that will knock a bitch out quick, so I choose to steer clear of their ass. Ketura and Heaven are the only women I've ever considered friends. With them being married to Saint and Cross, it makes us family.

Not only are we married to them, but we're also married to their cartel. Ketura and I have both been through some shit. Dealing with

Prentiss has been hard as hell. He has never looked at us as being worthy of being with his sons. Learning he felt some type of way about Heaven was no surprise me. I'm actually glad his old ass in jail. His possessive ways are detrimental to the St. Croix Cartel. Priest, Saint, and Cross run this shit better without his ass.

From the moment Priest stepped to me, I knew that with him I wanted forever. I was never the type of woman who played a blind eye to who he was. Priest wasn't a low-level drug dealer. He was the nigga to see to even be able to sell the shit. I knew that the bitches would be my biggest problem when we made shit official. He's always been the man that did his dirt but came home like it was nothing. Honestly, I became content with his bullshit as long as it never graced my doorstep. The elegant and luxurious lifestyle helped me to put the shit on the backburner.

After so many years of trying to block it out, the shit hit me full force. That's when I became resentful towards him. It wasn't until he started fucking with the bitch Keela that I lost my mind. This hoe was all over the city claiming to be his bitch. Shit got real funky when she called herself confronting me about my husband. I shot that bitch in her head right on my doorstep. One thing for sure and two for certain, I'm not arguing with no hoe about what the fuck belongs to me. The bitch caught me on the wrong day.

The shit was so crazy because I blanked out. I left her body on the porch until Priest came home. His ass was pissed that he had to get rid of the bitch. That was about a year ago. Ever since that incident, I've been on good bullshit with him in regards to his infidelity. I didn't realize just how resentful I was until one night he was asleep. I rolled over and got the urge to kill his ass. As much as I love Priest, my resentment towards him has put up this blockage that I can't seem to shake. Although I have forgiven him, I'm still in this place where I'm pissed off at him for his indiscretions.

The resentment that I've felt for a minute has caused me to have a lapse in judgment. I've done something that I know may cost me my marriage and possibly my life. Priest would never forgive me. At this point, I don't even forgive myself.

Priest coming home today showed me just how good of a man he is. Yes, he has done some things that have hurt me, but he has also done so many things that have helped me as a woman. He's an amazing father and provider. He would kill a brick and a building for me with no hesitation.

I shed tears as I ran my hand across the MacBook he got me. Just staring at my many journals with stories I had written depressed the fuck out of me. Before I could even start writing my truths, I had to handle some unfinished business. Being Mrs. Priest St. Croix is everything to me. It hurts me to know my resentment towards my husband has the possibility to strip me from the very title I've earned outright. My son and my daughter are my world, and I'm sure that I'm theirs. The decision I made is about to make all of our world crumble, and I have no one to blame but myself. I could have been stronger. Unfortunately, I gave into the worst type of temptation a married woman could ever give into.

The hardest thing about all of this is that I'm the wife that Heaven and Ketura look up to. I've always been the one that speaks on the importance of being the wife of a St. Croix. I could only imagine how they will look at me if this secret I'm carrying ever gets out.

━━━

Later that night, I laid in bed naked waiting for Priest to get out of the shower. It had been a minute since we were able to actually make love. I had been in my feelings, and he had been working around the clock trying to keep shit together for the family. Prentiss being locked up and on bullshit had my baby working overtime.

My pussy instantly got wet watching him walk out of the bathroom naked. Specks of water left behind after he dried off glistened off of his chiseled frame. His bald head shined from the overhead lights in our bedroom. He licked his lips as I parted my legs and started to play with my pussy.

"That's how you feel, huh?" He grabbed his long, thick dick and started to stroke it. It was something about the veins that protruded from his shaft that drove me crazy. Getting up on my knees, I crawled to the edge of the bed and licked all around the tip of his dick. Taking my time, I catered to every inch of it. Priest had his eyes closed with his head back. He knows I hated that shit. I liked for him to watch that dick disappear down my throat.

"Look at me, Priest!"

We locked eyes, and I went in for the kill, not long after he came down my throat. What I thought would be a night of pure love making turned out to be a full-blown fuck fest. Priest and I were fucking like animals. This nigga was putting the dick down and reminding me who the fuck he was. That good dick made a bitch fall in line real quick. Just being this moment with my husband lets me know everything I need is right here with him. Having my mind and heart in the right place gives me the motivation I need to handle my unfinished business.

———

"What y'all think about this one?" Heaven asked as she modeled another dress for the grand opening of her nail bar. She literally dressed down for everything. She needed to be dressed to kill for her opening.

"I love that one. It has your body looking right, sis."

"I agree with, Sheeda. Cross will lose his mind when he sees you in that." Ketura agreed. The red form-fitting Christian Dior dress looked beautiful on her.

"I hope I don't buss my shit trying to wear these damn heels. I don't see why I can't just get me a pair of Gucci pants and a shirt with matching sneakers." Heaven was hell-bent on wearing some damn sneakers, but I wasn't having that shit.

"These bitches be out here dressed for success. Atlanta is the new black Hollywood. Black women all over the city are opening up boutiques, restaurants, and nail salons. When you step out on the scene, you want people to know you're the baddest at this shit, not to mention Mrs. Cross St. Croix. Your name alone will bring in numbers. Trust me, lil sis, this dress, those red bottoms, and that big ass of yours will definitely turn heads."

"Thank you both so much for coming shopping with me. Let's go sit down and have some drinks. I'm hungry from all of this walking around. Plus, I'm stressed out behind these custody papers that I was served with this morning. Remy Ma's father is taking me to court for joint custody."

"You must have gold dripping from your pussy. That's the only thing I can think that it could to have that nigga playing with his life. Cross is going to end up killing that crazy fucker."

That nigga was some kind of crazy behind Heaven's ass. I'm so nosey that I started following his ass on IG. He is too damn fine to be as nutty as he is.

"That nigga is touched in the head for real," Ketura added.

"I've been knowing him damn near all of my life. It wasn't until recently he started to distribute this crazy ass behavior. Truthfully, I feel sorry for him because the shit is actually heredity. Apparently, his biological father was a couple of bricks short of a building. That's another damn story that is just too depressing to discuss. I'm more concerned about how Cross will take this news. He has enough on his plate with the things that are going on with his family. I just feel so bad about constantly burdening him with my baby daddy drama. The shit is not fair to him. Cross is too good of a man to have to deal with anything."

"It is so crazy hearing how highly you speak of Cross. I still can't believe his ass is married with a damn family."

"You and me both. I know you get tired of me telling you how happy we are to have you as our sister-in-law, but we really are."

"Thanks, Ketura. I'm happy you guys accepted me. For a minute I was worried with all the drama from his dad, but now I'm okay."

"Still keep your guards up, Heaven. Just because that mother-fucker is in jail doesn't mean shit. For all we know, he's in that bitch plotting on all of us. Stay woke at all time."

I be trying to keep it all the way one hundred with Heaven in regards to the St. Croix family. This shit is not always rainbows and damn unicorns. At the same time, it warms my heart to see just how much she and Cross love on each other.

"This bitch better not start no bullshit with me today. I swear I'm going to fuck her up!" Ketura said as we stood at that counter in Saks paying for the items we had. Looking across the store, it was Shayla and her whack ass crew.

"If Shayla knows what's good for her, she won't say shit to you. The bitch needed to be focused on trying to get her damn daughter back. If anything, she should be thanking God for you taking care of her daughter."

"Them hoes look like they're stealing. Don't even waste your time on that bitch. She's in here straight stunting in that outdated Gucci. Girl, look at them damn Givenchy slides. Them bitches so ran over she about to be walking barefoot in a minute."

"Heaven, your ass is crazy!" We were all laughing loud as happy. Them hoes instantly started looking and mean mugging."

"Laugh now, cry later!" Shayla yelled.

"Play crazy and get your ass killed. Keep it up, and I'm going to put your dead beat ass on child support. While you're in here, you need to be at home cleaning that nasty ass house up!"

Hearing Ketura yell that shit out in front of her crew had that bitch looking sick. Why? I don't know. Them hoes houses probably nasty as fuck too. Birds of a feather, flock the fuck together.

"Trifling hoe!" I made sure to add as we walked out of the store. We had stooped to that hoe level long enough.

As brave as a front Ketura was putting on, I knew to see that bitch hurt her. Shayla had given her husband the one thing she hadn't been able to. Having a baby is all she has ever wanted. I'm almost positive every day her heart breaks taking care of Sienna. At the same time, I bet it warms her heart in the sense that she gets to be a mother. Either way, I support whatever the fuck my sis wants to do with no judgment. Lord, knows I'm not in a position to judge anyone because my nose isn't clean. I'm walking around with a smile while I'm slowly dying inside.

After leaving Lennox Mall, we headed over to Old Lady Gang. After eating and having some drinks, we all parted ways. I should have taken my ass home, but instead, I ended up in the last place I should be. At the same, I needed to end this shit before my husband finds out that I've been having an affair with Angel Vargas, head of the Vargas Crime family and also a business associate of the St. Croix Cartel. If this shit gets out, there will definitely be bloodshed—starting with Priest murdering my ass. That's why I have to end this shit. I still can't believe I cheated on my husband with a nigga he does business with.

I was a ball of nerves as I rode the elevator up to Angel's penthouse suite in downtown Atlanta. This shit was like the ride of shame. Once the elevator came to a stop, I stepped off to a sexy ass Angel waiting for me.

"What do I owe this unexpected visit? You missed papi, huh?" He roughly pulled me inside of the suite and started kissing all over me.

"Stop, Angel. That's not why I'm here. We need to stop this shit. I'm getting things back on track with my husband. I just came over here to tell you that I can't do this anymore."

Angel just stared at me with them crazy ass Mexican eyes and laughed.

"I mean if you're going to just come here and tell me I can no longer have that sweet pussy, at least let me taste it one more time."

"No, Angel!" I put my hands up to protest, but his strong ass lifted me off my feet and basically threw me onto the sofa. In one swift motion, he reached underneath my skirt and basically ripped my damn panties off.

"Don't fight this shit!" Angel dropped to his knees and spread my legs apart before burying his long thick tongue inside my pussy."

"Shit! You have to stop Angel. We can't do this anymore!" I tried my best not to moan, but this nigga was a beast at eating pussy. I couldn't help but grab onto whatever I could and close my eyes while riding the waves of ecstasy.

"Nah, nigga! Don't stop! Keep eating that pussy! I want to see if it cums for you like it cums for me!" The sound of Priest's voice made me pop my eyes open. He was holding his gold Desert Eagle to the back of Angel's head.

"Please, Priest, I could explain!" My heart was racing, and I felt like I was about to pass out from sheer terror.

"Shut the fuck up before I put a bullet in your fucking head!

"Calm down!" Angel pleaded. That only made Priest angrier, so he struck him across the head with the butt of the gun.

"Nigga shut the fuck up and keep eating my bitch pussy like I said! You motherfuckers want to sneak behind my back I want y'all to do the shit in my face! Don't cry now, bitch! You weren't crying when you were fucking this nigga. I should have left your ass selling dime bags, you pussy ass hoe! Now keep moaning like you were at first!"

At this point, I was crying uncontrollably. The last thing I wanted was for Priest to make us do this sex act in front of him. He pressed the gun in the back of Angel's head. Blood was spewing out from where he hit his ass with the gun. Looking behind Priest, I locked eyes with Cross and Saint. It was one thing for Priest to see me in such a compromising position, but for his brothers to see me killed my existence.

"Please don't do this! I forcefully moved Angel's head from in between my legs. I tried to rush away, but Priest grabbed me by my hair and made me look at him. In that instant, Cross and Saint started beating the shit out of Angel.

"Open your mouth, bitch! Suck on this gun like you suck on that nigga's dick!" he gritted. Priest was so mad that he was foaming at the mouth like a rabid animal.

"I'm so sorryyyyyy!" He forcefully pushed the gun inside of my mouth. I felt like he had broken my jaw and some of my teeth.

"Hoe, you ain't sorry!" He quickly turned me around and pushed me away from him with so much force that I fell forward. At this time I watched in horror as Priest joined in beating Angel. The beating went on for so long. All I could do was lay on the floor and cry. I knew Angel was dead when Priest cut his tongue out his mouth and threw it at me. I immediately begin to gag looking at it.

"Ahhhh!" I screamed as Priest dragged me across the room towards the elevator.

"Get her the fuck out of here!"

"Should I take her to the estate, sir?"

"Absolutely not! That estate was built for my wife. Take her to the condo in Midtown where I take my hoes!"

Hearing Priest speak those words killed my soul. It felt like my heart stopped beating. The only reason I hadn't passed out yet was because his security was holding me up. Priest walked away from the elevator without a second look. I was numb on the ride to where the security was taking me. Life as I knew it was over, and I had no one to blame but myself.

———

It had been about two days since I had been at the condo Priest sent me to. I didn't have a purse or phone to call anyone. All I needed was to hear my kids' voice and to let them know that I'm okay. I've never been away from them for long periods of time without checking in, so I know they're probably worried about me.

The same guy that brought me here was standing guard and watching me like a hawk. This shit was scary because there was no telling what the fuck Priest was going to do with me. I had been staying up nonstop trying not to fall asleep, but I was exhausted.

I was so mad at myself for even going to see Angel. My stupid ass should have gone home and confessed. There is no coming back from this shit. How could I ever look at Priest or our kids again?"

I could only imagine what war I head started between the Vargas and St. Croix families. I should never have found solace in that man. Even though Priest had cheated on me, it won't be discussed. He caught me in the act, and that's all that matters at this point. I have no idea how anything good would come out of this.

After fighting my sleep, I finally was able to doze off, but it didn't last long. The smell of his Sauvage cologne invaded my nostrils and made me sit right up in the bed. He was dressed in all black holding his gun. He flamed up a blunt and sat back in the chair. The whole time he stared at me intensely.

"Please, Priest! Say something."

"Shut the fuck up! Just hearing your voice makes me want to murder you. I've been thinking of ways to kill you and get rid of your body, but my kids' face pop in my head every time I think about the shit. I want to beat the fuck out of you, but I'm not that type of nigga to put his hands on a woman, not even the bitch that betrayed me by fucking a nigga I did business with."

"I'm sorry. I was just so upset about you cheating on me with that bitch. I never meant for it to get out of hand. From the bottom of my heart, I didn't mean to hurt you. At the same time, you hurt me too, Priest. You cheated on me numerous times. I forgave you, and you're acting like I'm some whore!"

"That's because you are a whore. The difference between you and me is that you've never caught me in the act of fucking a bitch. Let's get some shit straight before you go trying to use my infidelities against me. I don't give a fuck what I do. You're a woman. You're supposed to carry yourself to a higher standard. I would have rather you left me for cheating instead of going to fuck another nigga."

"I know, Priest! Pleaseee, give me a chance to make this right. I want my marriage to work! " At this point, I had crawled out of bed and was kneeling in front of him on the floor.

"I can't even look at you right now. I've made other arrangements. I'll move into one of the other properties we own. I don't want to uproot the kids or be that father takes them away from you because I'm in my feelings. The house is all of yours. Of course, I'll make sure you're straight on the money side. You have access to the joint account. Don't call me for shit if it's not regarding my kids! Bitch, I don't want to see you or even hear your name being spoken in my presence." He stood to his feet and walked past me as I sat on the floor.

Getting the courage to gather myself and stand to my feet was hard as hell. Walking through the condo, I realized the security was now gone. On the coffee table sat my phone, car keys, and purse. I guess he thought enough of me to bring my things. That was my cue to head home to my kids. My Benz was parked in front of the building. Hopping inside, I cried all the way home. The ride on the highway was the longest it had ever been coming from Buckhead. Walking into my lavish home felt so different and empty.

"Good evening, Mrs. St. Croix. The kids are in bed, and they've had dinner. Is there anything you need from me before I retire to the guest house for the night?"

"No. Thank you, Irene." She looked at me with sympathy. Yeah, shit was all bad if the nanny felt sorry for me.

I headed up the stairs to check on my kids. They were both sound asleep. Walking inside of my bedroom reality set in. My husband would not be coming home. Looking inside his walk-in closet was the saddest sight. Everything was gone, including the hangers. His jewelry was gone as well. Heading into the bathroom, I wiped the tears that had fallen down my face. His side of the sink was also bare. Our bedroom looked as if he never even existed. Priest had left my ass, and I could do nothing about it.

CHAPTER SEVEN
HEAVEN

IT HAD BEEN three months since I moved to Atlanta, and I couldn't be happier. Life with Cross had been everything that I imagined it would be. I loved that even though he was always swamped with business, he made it a priority to check in with me throughout the day. Cross was so overprotective that I have to tell him to calm down. At the same time, I embrace it because some niggas don't give a fuck. I had been running around like a chicken with my head cut off trying to make sure the opening of my nail bar went smoothly. That added with gearing up for the custody hearing was driving me crazy.

Lil Dro and I hadn't been in contact since I left. He was literally the last person I wanted to talk to. However, after receiving the papers in the mail, I tried reaching out to him but found out he was locked up for beating the shit out of Shieka. How in the hell can he want joint custody and can't keep his ass out of trouble? I wasn't surprised though. That's Khiandre for you. I could imagine why he put his hands on her. Not that there is an excuse to do it, but I still want to know.

In about two weeks, I would be headed to Chicago for the court hearing. I pray Khiandre is out of jail so that we could come to some type of legal agreement. Although he pissed me off trying to fuck up my shit with Cross, I felt bad for keeping our daughter away for so long.

———

"Oh, shitttt!" Cross moaned as I slid up and down slowly on his dick. There was a time when riding him hurt like hell, but now I do that shit like a champ. I could feel my juices spilling out of me as I neared my climax.

"I'm cumming, baby! Oh my god!"

Cross grabbed my waist and started pounding roughly in and out of me until we both were climaxing. I couldn't believe I was doing this nigga dick like a pro. The bashful and sometimes shy Heaven was long gone. Meeting Cross was by far the best thing that ever happened to me. This nigga had awakened my inner freak and my third eye. Life with him was extremely different. If someone told me my daily routine would be meditating, burning sage, and smoking blunts, I would have told their ass they were lying.

"I think I just popped your ass off with twins. Who the fuck taught you to ride dick like that? He smirked as he smacked me on the ass and lifted me off of his dick.

"I taught myself, nigga."

We both laughed as he sat on the side of the bed and flamed up a blunt. I still hadn't told him about the custody hearing. I think right now would be the right time to tell him. He just had some good ass pussy, and now he was enjoying the afterglow. Yeah, this was the perfect time. Getting up from the bed, I went inside my top drawer and handed him the paperwork.

"I got this in the mail about two weeks ago. I'm sorry for just not giving it to you. I just know you've had a lot going on, and I didn't want to burden you with more of my baby daddy issues." Climbing back into the bed, I pulled the covers up over me and waited for him to respond.

"Heaven, I've told you to stop thinking that Remy Ma is a

burden. I love her just like I love my son. I don't give a fuck what is going on with this street shit or my family. You and the kids come first. I think this is good. You know I don't fuck with that bitch ass nigga period, but he's still Remy Ma's daddy. I'll head out there with you if you need me to. I love you, Heaven, and I support you to the fullest."

"I'm so lucky to have you in my life, Cross St. Croix." I straddled him and placed a juicy kiss on his lips.

"Nah! I'm the lucky one." I could feel his dick harden beneath me, so I did what any good wife would do. I let him slide in and kill my shit until I tapped out.

⌷⌷

It had been about a week since I heard from Rasheeda and I was starting to get worried. Cross, Priest, and Saint were all out of town on business. With Ketura not hearing from her either, we both got together and went over to her house. Something was definitely wrong. She loved social media, and she hadn't been posted or anything. So, yes, something was definitely wrong with her.

"If this bitch doesn't answer this gate. We're hopping over it." Ketura continued to buzz the gate, but no one was answering.

"I'm not jumping this big ass gate and fuck up my Balenciaga's! Bitch, you know I'm crazy about my gym shoes." Not only was I worried about my shoes, but I was also worried about breaking my damn neck. The damn gate was high as fuck. You would have to be Catwoman to get over it.

"This hoe see us at this gate too! Sheeda! Open this damn gate before we call the police over here!" Ketura was yelling into the intercom system. Just like that, the damn gate opened, and we drove up to the house.

I thought my house was the shit, but looking at Priest and Rasheeda's home, I needed a damn upgrade.

"This shit so dope! It reminds me of Roman times."

"Ain't it though. Priest ole weird ass loves Greek mythology."

Once we parked in front of the car, we hauled ass trying to get up to the door. Priest Jr. opened up the door and let us in.

"Hey, nephew. Where your momma at?"

"She in her room sad because my daddy moved out. I hope y'all came to make her happy because she is going through it." *This little girl needs her ass whooped.*

"What momma tell you about being grown and telling our personal business?" Priest Jr. was highly upset at Caprice for speaking like that, as he should be.

"Shut up, PJ!"

"No, you shut your grown ass up and go upstairs to your room!" Rasheeda yelled as she came down the stairs. I immediately felt sorry for her. I didn't even know what the hell was going on, but it was obvious shit was all bad.

"You okay, momma?"

"Yeah, son, I'm okay. Go up to your room so I can talk with Auntie Ketura and Heaven." He looked so concerned about his mother. I couldn't wait from Cross Jr. to get older and be protective of me.

"I'm sorry for not answering y'all calls I've just been going through. I'm not sure I can even tell either of you. I'm too embarrassed and ashamed. Come out on the patio. I don't want to risk my kids hearing me, especially that damn Caprice. I'm a second away from beating the skin off her grown ass. It's like since Priest moved out, she's gotten worse, and it hasn't been that damn long."

"Let me grab a bottle of Patrón before we head out there. I can tell we're going to need a drink for this shit." Ketura headed into the dining room and came out with a big ass bottle of Patrón and some shot glasses.

"It's a good thing I took some blunts from Cross' stash."

Reaching inside of my purse, I pulled out the blunts, and we all headed outside to sit on the patio. For a couple of minutes, we sat passing the blunt around and knocking back shots.

"Priest caught Angel Vargas eating my pussy in his penthouse suite."

I immediately started choking on the weed hearing her blurt that out. I was not expecting that.

"Oh my god! Bitch, I told you to dead that shit months ago."

"That's what I was trying to do. One thing led to another, and he had me laid out on the sofa eating the fuck out of my pussy. The shit happened so fast. Saint and Cross saw it too. That's why I'm super embarrassed. They beat Angel to death in front of me, and Priest cut his tongue out. I can't un-see that shit."

Rasheeda was now crying, and I couldn't do shit but move closer to comfort her. My ass was speechless. Here it was I thought I left this type of shit back home with my momma and her home girls. Lord, knows that some of them were some sneaky ass pussies back in the day.

"I'm just happy that he didn't kill your ass." Ketura knocked back a shot and removed some of the hair from Rasheeda's face that had fallen.

"He wanted to. That nigga forced his gun down my mouth with so much force that I thought he broke my damn jaw. I just wish I would have been stronger and didn't stoop to his level. He has cheated on me numerous times, and I forgave him. This one indiscretion on my part and he leaves. The nigga talked to me like I was a hoe on the street. I came home, and he had moved everything out. The nigga didn't even leave a sock behind by mistake. He won't even talk to me."

"Don't cry. He'll come around. Right now, his ego is bruised. It's crazy how niggas do us dirty all the damn time, but as soon as we do them dirty, all hell breaks loose. They kill me feeling betrayed. You got more heart than I do. Saint's ass brought a whole damn baby home, and I've yet to pop this pussy for another nigga, even though I'm well within my rights. I love you, and I love my bro Priest. At the same time, don't close yourself off from us. You need to call your momma. She has been going crazy."

"I spoke to her. The kids and I are going to go and stay with her for a little while. This house was built for all of us. With him not being here, I see no reason to stay. I've done all the crying I'm going to do. Thank you both so much for coming and check on me, but this is some shit I need to handle on my own."

"I'm not questioning your decision but taking the kids and going to the hood won't do shit but piss him off more."

"I doubt it. From the looks of it, he has moved on already."

Rasheeda handed us her phone, and I couldn't believe it. This nigga Priest was on IG posted with some bitch that looked just like Bernice Burgess. Her caption read *When Daddy comes to Miami*.

"This nigga Saint ain't shit either," Ketura added and swiped to the next picture. A big booty stripper was sitting on his lap while he smoked on a cigar.

I started swiping to see more pictures, and finally, Cross came into view. Bitches that barely had clothes on surrounded him. He was just posing and not touching, but I still didn't like the shit.

"So, much for being away on business," I said as I knocked back a shot.

This was officially my first time feeling some type of way about Cross in regards to other women. Technically, he wasn't doing anything, but he told me they were going for business and had no time to kick it. From the looks of it, they had more than enough time on their hands to kick it.

For the next hour or so, we all sat around knocking back shots and getting high. Regardless of how I felt about the picture, I was relieved that he wasn't actually touching the bitches. The more intoxicated I got, the more insecure I became. All I could think about is him being laid up with a bitch out in Miami. Quickly, I shook that shit from my mind. Cross has never given me a reason to be insecure, and I wasn't about to start now. The shit made me miss him even more, and I couldn't wait until he came home.

There was going to be so much more drama with Priest and Rasheeda. Her ass got drunk, broke her cell, and left the house with the kids. Ketura called Saint and told him she was about to bleach all his clothes. Later that night, I laid in bed and prayed that Cross and I never got to a point where we loved and hated each other at the same time.

"He was fine when I laid him down for his nap. When I went to check on him, he was turning blue."

I was crying and hysterical at the hospital. My son had stopped breathing in his sleep and I was losing my mind. Cross was still in Miami, and I needed him. I was freaking the fuck out. He was still struggling to breathe when we made it to the hospital.

"Stop crying, Heaven. The doctors have him stabilized and breathing. They're running test. Come over here and sit with me."

Mrs. St. Croix happened to be at the house helping out around the house per Cross' request. He swore I couldn't be home alone taking care of the kids. I was dead set against it, but was grateful for her being there with me. When I found my baby, I instantly panicked. My ass was so hysterical that I couldn't even give him CPR. She snatched him from me and went right into action resuscitating him.

"I cannot live if my baby dies. Jamaica, I will not survive another one of my babies passing away."

"That's enough! You will not speak death over my grandson. He is a St. Croix, and he will be just fine. Remember everything you speak negatively can manifest itself. We only speak positive things over this family. My grandson, Cross St. Croix Jr., will be just fine!"

Jamaica spoke so firmly, and I quickly calmed down. I needed to hear that because Lord knows I felt like I had no hope. When you lose a child, you lose a part of your mind that others don't understand. Jamaica and I walked back inside the room where my son was with the nurse who was checking his vitals.

"Hey, mom. We found out that your son had an asthma attack while sleeping. His oxygen levels are extremely low."

"I don't understand. He just had a five-month check-up, and everything was fine."

"That's the thing with asthma. It's extremely tricky, and you never know when an attack will come about. We're going to keep him a couple of days until we can get his oxygen levels up. Of course, you will have to follow up with his Pediatrician. We're going to be sending you home with meds, and of course, a breathing machine so that you can give him treatments."

"Okay. Thank you so much."

"See I told you he was going to be just fine." Jamaica wrapped her arms around me and hugged me tightly. At that moment, I was so happy to have her here with me. She made things so much easier.

My phone started to ring, and I knew it was my momma or my daddy. They had been calling me nonstop since I told them what was going on. When I answered the phone, I just wanted to let her know the baby was okay. Instead, she was telling me that someone had burned down my shop. The shit broke my heart. The devil was too damn busy for me. This shit happened at the wrong time. Here I am gearing up to open shop number three, and someone does this shit. With my son having a medical crisis and this happening to my shop, I decided to put the opening on hold.

———

"Don't cry, sis. I promise to rebuild it for you."

Lil Ace kept trying to get me to stop crying by assuring me he would rebuild. Amari was pissed as we walked around my first shop that they gave me. I think he was more upset than I was.

"I just don't understand who would burn my damn shop down. The Fire Marshall said an accelerant had been used to ignite the shit."

"I wonder if your bitch ass baby daddy is behind this shit," Amari said.

"He's in jail. I've already checked. Trust me. He was the first person I thought of. With him being in jail I'm lost as to who it could be at this point. I don't have beef with anyone, not even the bitch he had a baby with. This shit is literally a damn mystery.

"Don't even trip, sis. I promise we're going to find out and murder the motherfucker! Let's get the hell out of here. These damn fumes are starting to give me a headache," Lil Ace said as we all walked out of what used to be my shop.

I really wished Cross was here with me, but he stayed back with our son. Of course, I brought Remy Ma so that I could take her to see Lil Dro while I was here. The last thing I wanted was to take my baby to see her damn daddy behind bars, but she missed him.

"I love y'all. Thanks for coming. I'm going to sit here and wait for the company to come and board everything up."

"Nah, sis, we'll handle that! You go ahead and go see your people. I know this miss you. Make sure you go see, ma. She's been asking me all day about when your flights land. She's over at the other shop now."

"Thanks, bro. I'm about to head over there in a little while. I love y'all, and I'll check in with you later."

I hugged both of my brothers and hopped in my car to go see Madear. I missed that crazy ass old lady. She literally called both Cross and me all day every day.

As I drove a text message came through. Grabbing the phone and opening the text from Cross, I almost crashed looking at the picture of his fat ass dick. The shit had me ready to catch a flight back home to the dick. I don't know what had got into me. Since Cross came into my life, all I wanted to do was fuck. His ass would be sleep, and I would start sucking his dick just to wake him up and fuck. I loved being able to be so free with him. With him, I didn't have to fear being myself without judgment. Cross let me be me, and that's one of the main reasons that I fell in love so quick. I only had to be out here a couple of more days, and then I could go home to my man. I haven't been out here in Chicago a full twenty-four hours and was ready to take my ass back to Atlanta to be with my husband.

Pulling up to Madear's house, I was not surprised to see them partying on a damn weekday. It was summertime in the Chi, and every day of the week was a party. That's just how Chicagoans are. The west side did their thing, and the south side did theirs. No matter what part of the city you come from, it was sure to be a party on one block, and a shootout on the next block.

"Look at my grandbaby! You went and married that nigga from the south, and he got you glowing. Maybe I need to go down south and get me a boo!"

I hugged her and then kissed my granddaddy on the cheek. I missed these crazy fools.

"Get your ass whooped out here, Sherita!" I was shocked to hear my granddaddy Dino snap. He usually lets Sherita cut a fool.

"Don't start that shit today. I'm going to put both you nutty moth-erfuckers off my property. Hey, Heaven baby."

"Hey, Madear. What you cook?"

"I didn't cook anything. Your grandma made some shit that's supposed to be fried chicken and rice. She put that damn chicken in some type of batter, and it looked a hot mess. All the damn crust fell off the damn chicken. The rice is so damn gummy it doesn't make no sense."

"It can't be that bad, Madear," I said, laughing.

"The hell it ain't. My dog didn't even want that shit. Go in there and look at it. If she stops drinking and chain-smoking, she might be able to cook a damn decent meal."

"Don't you go judging me. You smoke more weed than a little bit."

"Dealing with y'all I have to smoke my joints."

I just stood in the middle of them as they argued, and I was happy to be home. This was what I'd known my whole life with them. It's like a breath of fresh air to come home to the craziness. Living in

Atlanta with Cross and his family was always serious and never any laughter, with the exception of him and I laughing and joking with one another. Sometimes people complain about their dysfunctional relatives, but not me. These people keep me going.

"I just stop by to see y'all for a little while. I'm about to get Remy Ma from Khia and Dro, and then head over to my house."

"You still got your house here. I thought you put it on the market?"

"No granddaddy. My father bought me that house, and I will never sell it. Plus, it's good that I still have it. I don't have to pay to stay at a hotel when I come to visit."

"Your ass is rich, stop being cheap! Now, what you should do is leave the key with your Aunt Gail and me. We could make some damn money throwing old school parties on the weekend."

"Absolutely not, grandma! Y'all friends don't know how to handle their liquor. I'll come home and won't have a damn house. I love you with all my heart, but ain't no way I'm giving you gang members access to my house." Sherita had lost her mind.

"Granddaddy heard about somebody burning your shop down. Now you know back in my day I used to hang with Foe nem. If you need the gang and me to handle that shit, say the word. I got my little niggas on deck."

It took everything in my power not to laugh at Dino. He and my granny Sherita had the jokes today.

"I already know how you and your people get down. I'm good though. My daddy is Remy Ramirez, and my husband is Cross St. Croix. Trust me. They're going to find out who did it. In the meantime, go help your wife. She's falling, and she can't get up."

I couldn't help but laugh at Sherita she had tried to do a split and was stuck. No matter how much time passes, this family will forever be bat shit crazy. Before getting in my car and pulling off, I made sure to take a picture of Sherita and send it to my momma.

"Since when you start cooking?" My mother was in the kitchen cooking a feast, and that was rare. Rose' don't do no cooking unless it's a special occasion.

"Don't come in my damn house insulting me little girl. I actually missed your ass, so I decided to cook you a home-cooked meal. I've made dressing, smothered turkey wings, baked macaroni, greens, and cornbread."

"Daddy must be hitting it right because them all his favorites."

I couldn't do nothing but laugh at my momma. Ever since the last fight her and my daddy had, she's been on her best behavior. She's been staying home and being the good little wife.

"Take your ass back to Atlanta!" She threw the towel at me, and I tried to dodge it.

"I'm sorry, ma. Thank you so much. I really appreciate it. I'm going to take mine to go because I have to get up in the morning and go to the county."

"What the hell you have to go to the county for?" My mother was staring me down with them judgmental eyes. I was already aware that she was not going to agree with me taking Remy Ma to see Lil Dro.

"I'm going to take Remy Ma to see her daddy. What you don't think I should?"

"What I think doesn't matter? I'm stepping back like you want Heaven. You're a grown ass woman with kids and a husband. If you think taking her to see her father is cool, then do it. I'm your mother, and I support any decision you make."

My momma was so full of shit. She knows damn well she doesn't want me to take Remy Ma to see Khiandre. Since she was minding her business, I was going to let her be. It's not often she allows me to make my own decisions. Instead of pushing the issue, I decided to change the subject.

"Where is daddy?"

"He had to make a run with your Uncle Thug. Don't tell him I told you this, but I think them fools out there trying to find out who burnt your shop down."

"I still don't know why anybody would do that. I'm not beefing with anyone, so I'm lost as to why someone would do that."

"Listen, baby. You don't have to be beefing with anyone. Right now, you're the talk of the town. You overcame what was sent to break you. Heaven, you have a nigga that loves the fuck out of you, not to mention he's a motherfucking boss. You're an overnight entrepreneur and success story. What you've accomplished in a matter of months, women can't do their whole lives. Know and understand it's a lot of bitches walking around with dim ass light-bulbs, and they want to unscrew yours. Heaven Acearia Ramirez- St. Croix, you're shining bright baby! These hoes hate it.

Just know you have your family behind you one hundred percent. If we have to get out there and rebuild that shop with our bare hands then so be it. In the meantime, do you have your gun on you? I want you to keep it on you at all times. I'm surprised Cross didn't send a damn army out here to watch over you."

"Yes, I have Come here. Let me show you something." I grabbed her hand and basically pulled her to the living room to look out of the window.

"See that black Lincoln Town Car? That's the security detail that he thinks I don't know he has following me around. My husband does not play about me."

"I know that shit's right. Come on, let's eat and sip on this wine." Walking back into the kitchen, I sat on one of the barstools as she fixed our plates and poured the glasses of wine.

"Thank you so much, ma. I've missed you so much. Life is so good in Atlanta with Cross. The only thing is I get homesick sometimes. Atlanta is a world away from Chicago. I be missing my dawg Yah-Yah like crazy. Don't get me wrong Ketura and Rasheeda are so cool, and they really be showing me the ropes. It's just different with Yah-Yah and me. I guess because we're closer in age. They aren't that much older. It's just that I see them going through so much with Saint and Priest. I'm not trying to be disrespectful, but I see them going through the things that you and my aunties went through. I don't know. It's just that I can't relate because Cross and I don't have those problems. We're good on all levels."

"Of course, you're good on all levels. You're newlyweds. It's still the honeymoon stage. Trust me the arguments and fights will come. I'm not pouring salt on your relationship. At the same time, if you're not fighting with your mate, there is a problem. When I say that what I mean is when you fight with your mate over something, it means there is a sense of care. If you're walking around acting like shit doesn't affect you, or if you're walking around staying quiet to keep the peace, that's a recipe for disaster because shit is sure to hit the fan. Listen to your momma, baby girl. Being in love with a kingpin is not easy, but a real bitch with heart can do it. You have that heart, and you have it because of the blood running through your veins.

I met the man you know as your father the day I walked out of prison from doing a four-year bid behind a man that never loved me. One look at his fine ass and he had me gone. He offered me a job at his club and made sure I kept money in my pocket. One day your biological father kidnapped you and me from Chuckie Cheese. He raped me anally as punishment for not wanting to deal with him. I passed out, and when I came to, I was a bloody mess.

He had kidnapped you, and I was lost. I didn't know where else to run but to Remy— not knowing where you were had me freaking out. I rushed into that man's office, and a bitch was on her knees giving him head. That sight broke my heart. He wasn't my nigga, but in that moment of seeing him, I knew that I wanted him. I took off running, and he came after me. That's when he found out what Ace did to me. I was too ashamed to go to the hospital. That man laid me down and examined me to see how bad the damage was. The moment he placed soft kisses on my ass cheeks let me know he was cut from a different type of cloth. Long story short, we got you back, thanks to Diamond dropping you off to the club.

From that moment until now, that man has taken care of us. You have witnessed firsthand the fights and the arguments. Hell, just recently we were on the verge of divorce. Momma is telling you this because no matter the fairytale we get from these powerful ass men that we love, a broken heart here and there comes with the territory. Cross is a good man. He reminds me so much of your father. That's why I have no qualms about you being with him. I can proudly say that is my son-in-law.

Cross holds himself to a higher standard, and he expects the same from you. So, certain shit he will not let slide. I say all that to say, don't walk around with the idea that marriage will always be rainbows and sunshine. There will be a lot of storms you will have to endure. I'm only telling you this because the first fight your father and I had almost made me die. No one in this world could tell me my husband had a mean streak in him. Had my soft ass crying for weeks, but our love didn't change. Momma just wants you to be prepared for anything. I love you, Heaven."

"I love you too, ma. Thanks for the advice and the dinner."

We exchanged hugs, and for the rest of the evening, we chilled. It was the first time in my life that I actually smoked weed and got tipsy with my mother. I would definitely cherish the moment forever. As a wife and mother, I walked away looking at marriage in a different light. My mother had told me so many funny and sad stories about her marriage. Things I don't think I could live through. Then again, after everything I've learned from her, I know that could overcome anything.

<hr>

There was nothing but silence between Dro and I as we sat in a private visitation room. He played and loved on Remy Ma as I sat quietly observing. As I sat across from him, I felt nothing. He was the daughter of my father, nothing more. I didn't even feel pain or anger behind the things he put me through. The only thing I was still mad about was him showing up at my wedding cutting the fuck up. With knowing that it wasn't a planned hit that he had nothing to do with, I decided to let it go. The smile on my daughter's face let me know she was happy to see her nutty ass daddy.

"I just want to say thank you for bringing my daughter to see me. You might not believe it, but I miss her so much."

"You miss her so much that you're sitting your ass in jail. What the hell, Khiandre?"

He put his head down in shame, and he should be ashamed of himself. Khiandre should be tired by now with putting himself in these crazy ass situations.

"I know, Heaven. That's why I don't want to take you to court for custody. The main reason I've been doing a lot of fuck shit is because I couldn't bear to see you with someone else. I went to Cali and came home on a mission to get my family back only to find out you were pregnant and getting married to that nigga Cross. I showed up at your wedding to crash that motherfucker. The only reason my plan fell through was because them niggas were there with an agenda on their own.

The custody thing was out of anger. A nigga felt like you took my daughter and gave her to that nigga. Then I realized you were happy, and it had nothing to do with me. With everything that has happened, I know that you now have everything that I never gave you. You deserve happiness, even if it isn't with me. I'm sorry for everything that I've done to you and my daughter. It took for me to sit back and realize just how fucked up of a nigga I've been to you. I've been doing to you what my father did to my mother. Cross is only doing for Remy Ma what Big Dro did for me. It's just a shame so much shit had to transpire for me to see the bigger picture.

I've already told my lawyer to stop the custody proceedings. I'll be moving to Cali to take on some business ventures that I have out there. Remy Ma can come see me for holidays and possibly the summer. Of course, we still have to deal with the logistics, but I assure I'm not on any more bullshit. I apologize for everything.

There's no need to accept my apology right now. The best apology I can give you is showing you that I want to be a good father."

For the first time, I wholeheartedly believed Lil Dro. His eyes were different from the other times he swore he was going to do right.

"The ball is in your court. However, I must ask why you whooped Sheika's ass." I spoke underneath my breath but loud enough for him to hear. I didn't want to risk anyone else hearing our conversation.

"Let's just say that hoe's a snake, and she's disappeared with my son. For the sake of her life, she better stay gone. On a brighter note, I met someone when I was down in Cali. Her name is Chynna White. While out there, we did our thing, and she's getting ready to give birth to my twins. I'm only telling you this because as the mother of my daughter, you deserve to know her. Before I move out to Cali, I would love for you to have a sit-down with her and introduce Remy Ma. Of course, I respect your wishes if you're not feeling it. Just think about it. Our time is almost up, so just think about it. Thanks for bringing my baby girl to see me."

"I'll think about it, Khiandre."

I'm almost positive there was more to what happened with him and Shieka. At the same time, it wasn't my business. As far as this new bitch goes, I don't really care to meet her. I haven't even decided if I'm going to allow my daughter to go clear across the country to California. I'll cross that bridge when I come to it.

After leaving the visit, I couldn't wait to get home to my son and my husband. My mother begged me to let my daughter stay and spend time with them since it was the summer. I know she missed them too, so I let her stay. That would give Khia and Big Dro time with her as well. On the plane ride home, I sat in anticipation for the moment I laid my eyes on Cross. I missed him so much. A bitch was going through dick withdrawals, and I needed my fix.

Surprised wasn't the word for the way I was feeling. When my flight landed, I just knew that Cross would be outside waiting to pick me up, but he wasn't. I called, and he basically told me that he was busy. I literally sat at the airport for a minute before I took a taxi. Pissed wasn't the word because we lived far as hell from the airport. I wanted to give in and call Rasheeda or Ketura, but I decided not to.

When I made it home, I was so happy to see my baby. He looked so much better since his health scare. It was still scary to know that he had to do daily breathing treatments. Now that I know he has asthma, I know how to control it.

"Welcome home, Mrs. St. Croix," Bentley said as he came and grabbed my suitcase.

"Thank you. Was CJ good for you and Ms. Bam?"

"Absolutely. We had maybe once or twice. Mr. St Croix has been here around the clock since you've been gone. We only had him because we made him get some air. I think he's crazier than you are behind that baby."

I smiled hearing him say that, not that I was surprised because Cross is absolutely crazy about our son.

After a long stressful couple of days in Chicago, all I wanted to do was sleep. After showering and getting my baby ready for bed, I snuggled with him in bed. Sleep was not coming easy. My ass was tossing and turning like crazy. Cross wasn't answering his phone, and I was worried about him. That and the fact that it was past three in the morning had me losing my mind. This wasn't like him not to answer his phone, and he's always been home at a decent hour. My ass couldn't take it. I tracked his phone and came up with the location. I got dressed and headed over to the location.

With me not being familiar with Georgia, the shit was scary, but I made it. The address was that of a big ass mansion. The many cars and people all out let me know it was a mansion party. The shit was gated, and I had to pay the damn security two hundred to get in. I wasn't mad. I would pay whatever to find my nigga. I wasn't a groupie. I was a wife on a mission.

It didn't take me long to find Cross. For the first time, I saw him in a different form. He was Cross St. Croix, not Cross the gentleman that took me on a date amongst the clouds in Dubai.

Disgusted wasn't the word for what I felt. Strippers were entertaining Cross, Priest, and Saint. The room was filled with nothing but bitches' shaking their asses, and it was raining money. Observing Cross making it rain on a bitch and smack her on the ass angered the fuck out of me. I almost fell trying to get over to him, but security stepped in front of me.

"You better move your big ass out of my way!" I tried pushing pass him, but his big ass wasn't budging.

"I'm sorry, ma'am. I can't let you in the section."

"If you don't want me to start shooting in this bitch, you better go over there and tell Cross his wife is outside!" My gun was in my car, and I had every intention of letting bullets fly if he didn't come out. I walked out quick as hell in an effort to not to act a plum fool in this motherfucker.

"Cross, let you out to play, huh? Here I thought I was gone be able to suck that dick tonight." I look back, hearing a familiar voice. Just as I thought, it was the bitch from the hookah lounge. Why this hoe wanted to try me at this time, I didn't understand. My car was steps away, so I didn't say shit to the hoe. When I made it to my car, I grabbed my gun from the glove compartment. Taking a deep breath, I swiftly walked back over to where the bitch was with her friends talking shit.

"What you say, bitch? Repeat that shit! Hoe, speak up! You had a lot to say a minute ago." I had my gun pointed at her ass, and she was trying her best not to look scared, but I could smell the fear radiating off of her ratchet ass.

"It ain't that serious over Cross! Trust me, bitch!"

"It's very fucking serious. You the same bitch that was just popping shit about sucking my man's dick! Pop that slick shit now."

"What the hell are you doing, Heaven?" Cross asked.

"I'm handling some business. Ain't that what you're out doing?"

"Give me this damn gun. Your ass is wilding." He snatched the gun from me with so much force that he almost broke my damn arm.

"Cross, you better let that hoe know she ain't in Chicago no more! We gets it cracking in the south too."

"Shut the fuck up before I let her shoot your dumb ass!"

Cross pushed me towards my car, not with force but with just enough to make me move forward. I was pissed because I really wanted to shoot her ass. This was her second time with that disrespectful shit.

"Fuck is you doing here, Heaven? Where is my son?" Looking at Cross, I could tell he was pissed.

"Our son is at home with Ms. Bam. I'm here because you aren't answering your phone. You told me you were handling business. What I saw in that house was not business. Since when did we start staying out late and lying?"

"Go home, Heaven. I'm not the nigga that puts his personal business in the streets. We'll talk when I get home." This nigga handed me my gun and walked off.

Cross was so calm, but angry at the same time. For a minute I was stuck standing there not really sure of what had just happened. Looking around, I could see that people were standing around staring at me. The hoe Ari and her friends were enjoying this shit. On my dead son, I swear I'm beating her whenever I see the bitch again. Instead of embarrassing myself further, I jumped in my car and took my ass home.

The moment I made it home, I headed right out on the patio to smoke a blunt. My ass needed to calm down. I was trying to understand why Cross was acting the way that he was. Not long after, I could hear his music blasting as he pulled up to the house. Everything inside of me wanted to rush inside the house and go the fuck on him as soon as he stepped inside. Instead, I acted nonchalant, just like he just did. The way he walked off on me is what angered me the most. How dare he do that shit in front of that bitch. The more I sat and thought about it, the angrier I became. Once I faced the whole blunt, I went inside of the house in search of Cross. Entering the bedroom, I found him in bed with our son watching TV. With me just getting done smoking, I took a quick shower before climbing in bed. I didn't want my son to inhale any of the smoke from my clothing.

After showering, I walked back into the bedroom, and Cross was looking at *SportsCenter*.

"So, you're going to act like everything is cool?"

"Go to sleep, Heaven."

"I'm not sleepy, Cross. I need to know why the fuck you acting like you mad or don't give a fuck about what just happened."

"Lower your tone and watch your mouth. I'm acting cool about the situation to keep from beefing with my wife. Lay your ass down and forget the shit."

"Nah! Ain't no forget the shit. I just walked in a house and saw your hands all over a bunch of nasty ass bitches! You lied to me and said you were out on business."

Before I knew it, Cross jumped out of bed in nothing but his boxers. The nigga was looking good as fuck, and for a minute, the dick print had me blinded.

"Since you insist on bringing me out of character, let's get some shit straight. I was out handling business. That party was for an associate of ours that we're trying to solidify some shit with, not that I have to tell you shit or explain shit to you. Last time I checked, you were walking around this motherfucker making decisions like you're a single woman."

"What the hell are you talking about, Cross?"

"I'm not talking about shit, but I'm sure your bitch ass baby daddy had a lot to say when you visited that nigga!" Cross stepped closer in my face, and I could feel the heat of anger radiating off of him.

"That's why you're acting like this? I took Remy Ma to see her father. What the fuck was so wrong about that?"

"The fact that you don't see a problem with the shit is a problem for me! Maybe marriage is not your thing! A bitch in the street would know that she is not supposed to go see her ex in jail. I don't give a fuck if that is her baby daddy. Somebody else could have taken her. The fact that you didn't have the common decency to at least check with your husband lets me know you're fucked up in the head, Heaven! One thing about me is that I need a woman that uses her mind at all times. You know the history with that nigga and me, not to mention the nigga is not to be trusted. For you to be so cool with going to see him got me thinking you still got feelings for the nigga! If that's the case, let me know now. The ink ain't yet dried on the marriage license. We can get the shit annulled my love. It's a line around the corner of bitches dying to Mrs. Cross St. Croix!"

Cross pushed pass me like he hadn't just crushed my entire existence. His words really hurt my feelings. My hurt feelings mixed with the embarrassment I felt was cause for the ugly bitch cry. The tears fell so rapid I had to run into the bathroom and cut the water on to stifle my cries. He was absolutely right. I should have known better, but all that extra shit he said wasn't right. If he was trying to hurt me, he succeeded. That was downright disrespectful for him to even speak about our marriage way. The shit was wrong on many levels.

After crying my eyes out, I finally got the courage to just go to bed. Had I known he was going to go so damn hard on me, I would have laid down and taken my ass to sleep like he told me to do. Climbing into bed, I tried waiting for him to come back to bed. The least I can do is woman up and apologize for my fuck up. I waited in vain because he never came back to bed. Cross and I were officially having our first fight, and I hated it.

The next morning I woke up pissed that he never came to bed. To make matters worse, he left without saying a word. Granted he had a right to be upset with me, but he didn't have to carry this shit the way that he was. Being married to Cross St. Croix was everything, but being married to Heaven Ramirez was a gift from God. Cross has me gone, but not gone to the point where I'm going to allow him to think he can play with me like this.

Instead of sulking and being all sad, I decided to get out of the house. Rasheeda's mom was throwing a big barbecue, and she invited me. I made sure to get cute and head my ass right on over there. Granted I didn't know her people but there was no sense in me sitting my ass at home in my feelings. I might be adding fuel to the fire, but whatever. Cross is mad at me anyway.

⊏⟩

"Bitch, the drug dealers are out here!' Ketura said as we passed a blunt back and forth.

What I thought was a simple backyard family gathering was actually a block party. At any minute, I just knew it was going to be a shootout. As I sat back with Ketura in the lawn chairs in front of Rasheeda momma's house, I observed her in rare form. Rasheeda knew all of the hood niggas.

"I can' believe her ass over there shooting dice with all them niggas."

"Listen, these are her people. Before she met Priest, she lived that hood life. Being married to him slowed all of that hood shit down. Trust me. This is her element.

"I see. Her ass is fucking them up on the dice." Rasheeda ass looked like a whole nigga. Gone was the damn designer gear she rocked. She had on a basic jogging suit with gym shoes.

"Y'all good over here?"

"Yes," we said unison to Rasheeda's mom, Rashay.

"Okay. Let me know if y'all need something. I'll be over here at this dice game taking Rasheeda's motherfucking money. I taught her everything she knows." We both laughed as she headed over to join the dice game.

"They asses are like two peas in a pod. Rasheeda is just like her momma."

Before I could answer, an incoming call from Cross flashed across my phone screen. I decided to ignore his ass just like he ignored me.

"Answer that phone, Heaven."

"Nope. I'm giving him a taste of his own medicine. I still can't believe he never answered the phone for me."

"I suggest you be the bigger person. If you don't answer that phone, that nigga is gone roll up here. I promise you don't want them problems. Saint is mad at me right now, so he's not coming over this way. Trust me. If we weren't into with each other right now, I wouldn't even be out here. I'm sure that's why Cross is calling. As a matter of fact, let me go tell Rasheeda we're about to go. Sitting and thinking about it that nutty motherfucker might knock my head off my shoulders when I get home." I just shook my head at Ketura as she walked over to the dice game.

"Damn, ma, you beautiful as fuck! You not from around these parts, are you?" He stroked my leg, and I quickly pushed his hand away!

"Don't touch me."

"I don't mean any disrespect, ma. I see you with that fat ass rock on your finger, and I know the pussy must be good to that nigga. Let me give you my number just in case that nigga fuck up."

"No. Thank you." I quickly got up and got away from his ass. He was staring at my ring hard as hell. He looked like a damn jackboy.

I texted Ketura and Rasheeda and let them know that I was leaving. Getting in my car, I tracked his phone and found out he was at his car dealership. Hopping on the highway, I headed straight over there. I decided that I needed to be the bigger person and apologize. After all, he never would have said those things to me had I not went to see Lil Dro.

It didn't take me long to make it to the dealership. Cross had nothing but exotic cars lined up on the lot. My baby was an entrepreneur. It's so amazing that he pushes bricks for a living as well. One would never know by just looking at him. Cross carries himself like a boss.

"Good evening, Mrs. St. Croix."

"Hello, Anita." As I spoke to his secretary, I headed to his back office.

Walking inside, I saw that he was on the phone so I took a seat across from him. I waited quietly as scrolled through my IG. My followers were up tremendously. All of the staff that I had were so dope and talented. With one of the shops being burned down, I had to shift some of my workers. It made me feel good to be able to keep on the payroll even though the shop was down. Just thinking about my shop being burned down is disheartening. It was driving me crazy not knowing who the fuck would want to do that shit.

Looking up from my phone, I locked eyes with Cross. I was so into my phone that I didn't realize he was done talking.

"What's good?" he spoke casually as he rested his index finger in his temple. This man was sexy as fuck no matter what mood he's in.

"I just came to apologize for not being respectful as your wife. Going to see Lil Dro without even talking to you about it was disrespectful. I'm sorry for coming to the party and wilding like that."

He sat stoically just staring at me. I should have known he wasn't going to let me off that easy. His demeanor was pissing me off. Instead of sitting there continuing to look stupid, I just jumped up to leave. I took giant steps heading out of the office. Of course, he was on my stopping me from walking off.

"Heaven, bring your ass back here! Why the fuck are you walking off?"

"Cause! You're acting like you're so mad at me. I'm sitting here trying to apologize and make things right. You're not saying anything, you just looking at me. Why you be acting all nonchalant like it's fuck me?"

I was mad at myself for crying right now. I'm at a place in my life where I want to be stronger when it comes to certain shit. This wasn't even worth crying over. It was mediocre compared to what other women had been through.

"Stop crying. I accept your apology. Make this the last time you do some shit without thinking about me first. You know how I am. I'm sorry for the shit I said to you last night. That shit was so wrong and out of pocket. There is a lot of shit I question, but our marriage isn't one of them. I'm sorry, baby. I was speaking out of anger. You forgive me?"

"Of course, I forgive you." Cross wiped my face and kissed me on the lips. I couldn't help but wrap my arms around him as tight as I could.

"I love your crybaby ass."

"Stop laughing, Cross. You know I'm soft-hearted. It's your fault for being such a gentleman to me. My ass can't take it when you mad. That shit has me all in my feeling. Seriously, on some real shit, I am sorry. Going to that jail was wrong, and from the bottom of my heart, I never meant to make you look at me differently. When I said "I do" I meant that shit, Cross. There ain't another nigga out here in this world for me."

"That's real, and I'm glad you let me know how you really feel. It gives a nigga the reassurance he needs. I'm actually done here. Let's go get something to eat and some drinks. It's been a minute since we spent time together.

"I have to go home and get dressed first. I wore this over to Rasheeda momma's barbecue and I smell the smoke on my clothing."

"Speaking of that motherfucking barbecue, make sure that's your last time over in the damn hood. You have on an eighty thousand dollar ring, and the nigga that was in your face was trying to get more than pussy. He's a well-known jackboy, and he was targeting you. I'm happy you decided to get in your car and leave. Let's get something straight. You're my wife. I have no say so in what Ketura or Rasheeda does, but you belong to me. A lot of shit is about me protecting you, so don't get it confused with me being possessive. Being out here is all new to you. I really don't like you all out driving around and shit by yourself. It's not safe. Please allow Bentley to take you around when I can't. Motherfuckers are grimy, and you're like a golden ticket to these niggas. Once they find out whose wife you are, they'll start plotting. You aren't married to a regular nigga, but you know that already. I just want you to move more cautiously and pay attention. Go ahead home and get dressed. I'll be there shortly."

Cross and I engaged in a passionate kiss before I rushed out to head home. It was like a weight was lifted off my shoulders. The walls felt like they were closing in when we were in a bad space. I hauled ass getting home because I couldn't wait to go out on our date.

Pulling into the driveway, I hopped out of the car and tried rushing towards the door. Before I could make it to the door, a masked man came out of nowhere.

"Ahhhhh!" I screamed as the person tried to cover my mouth. I bit the fuck out of their hand.

Everything moved so fast it was like a movie. One minute I was tussling with the person. The next I heard I gunshot go off. It wasn't until I felt pain in my upper chest that I knew I had been shot.

CHAPTER EIGHT
CROSS

MY MIND WAS all over the place trying to get to the hospital. Hearing something happened to Heaven had me about to lose my mind. My family wouldn't tell me anything, and that made the shit worse. A nigga didn't even understand what the fuck had happened. She just left me. The whole ride to the hospital, I was feeling fucked up. Lately, I had just been letting her go out freely. The last thing I wanted was for her to feel like a caged animal out here. She wasn't herself being so far away from her people. She always acted like she was cool, but I know she was lying. Now some shit has popped off behind me letting her be out alone. I'm going to lose my fucking mind if she's not okay.

Walking inside of the emergency entrance, the first person I saw was my mother.

"Where's she at, ma?"

"Calm down. We don't know what's going on. We're waiting for them to tell us something. They brought her in about twenty minutes ago, so I'm sure someone will be coming out soon." My mom was trying her best to come me down, but I couldn't.

"How the fuck am I supposed to calm down? Somebody shot her!

I'm telling y'all right now, I'm going to burn this city the down behind my wife!"

"This ain't the place for you to be talking like that, bro?" Priest pulled me away from my OG and walked me out of the emergency room. As soon as we got outside, Saint was walking up.

"Is my son, good?"

"Yeah, bro. Ketura has him. Ms. Bam and Bentley are okay. They stayed back at the house to clean up after the police left. What are they saying about, Sis?"

"Shit, we still waiting for them to come out and say something. Let's get back in here and see what's going on, bro. Keep that other shit on the low. You know them crackers waiting to catch one of us up. You already know it's about to bloodshed around this motherfucker. Right now, you have to keep calm and make sure Heaven is good before we start terrorizing the fucking city." Priest was holding me by my shoulders trying to calm me down.

"I know bro. What am I going to do if she doesn't make it? Who in the fuck would be so damn bold to come on my property? What bitch ass nigga think it's so sweet he could hit her up. That's my baby! That's my world! My purpose! My motherfucking heaven on earth! You better believe I'm going to paint this bitch red!"

Walking away from my brothers, I walked back to the emergency room. My mother was talking to a doctor. I rushed getting over to where they were.

"Here, he is. This is her husband."

"What's going on with my wife?" I got straight to the point.

"Mrs. St Croix is very lucky to be alive. The bullet that hit her went in and out of her shoulder without causing any major damage. She does have a concussion from hitting her head on the pavement. I'm going to keep her a couple of days just to make sure that she's going to be okay. I'll send her home with pain meds, and in a couple of weeks, she should be normal. Right now, she's out of it, but you can come back later and visit. " I breathed a sigh of relief hearing him say that she was okay.

"Thank you so much, doc." I shook the man hand so hard that I probably hurt his old ass.

"That's what up, bro. I knew sis was hard body," Priest said as him and I dapped up, followed by Saint and I doing the same.

"I'm going to get ma home. Then, I'm going to check on Ketura and the kids. When you leave this hospital, we need to get this shit popping. Fuck talking. We are past that shit. I'm ready to get shit popping. "

"I'm with you, bro. We'll meet back up. I need to go get Rasheeda from the Bluff before I have to murder her ass. She got my kids down there like this shit cool!"

"Yeah, you do that because I'm tired of your ass playing "Contagious". I was about to start calling your ass Mr. Biggs around this motherfucker!" Saint said as he walked off.

Priest didn't find that shit funny, but it was funny as fuck. I wanted to laugh bad as hell, but right now wasn't the occasion. That nigga has been all in his feelings behind catching Rasheeda with that nigga Angel. I was hurt for him. The nigga is better than I am because I would have murdered her ass too. At the same time, I don't know what would happen had I caught Heaven letting a nigga eat her pussy. Then again, let me stop lying. Her people would be picking out a plot and I would be getting fitted for an orange jumpsuit. A nigga was going to prison behind that pussy.

After everyone left, I headed to Heaven's hospital room. She was sound asleep and looking beautiful as ever. She didn't even look like she had got shot earlier in the day. I placed a kiss on her lips and sat down in the chair next to her bed. It was mind-boggling how someone so innocent is subjected to so much shit. Kissing the back of her hand, I made a vow to kill the motherfucker that hurt her. Heaven didn't deserve the shit she had been through. I was feeling fucked up because I'm supposed to protect her. She was never supposed to be by herself. The one day I give security the day off, this shit happens, which tells me that a motherfucker had been following her around. Nothing kicked off when she had security. It didn't take a rocket scientist to see that she was the intended target.

———

The next morning I woke to see Heaven sitting up and eating. My ass must have been tired because I slept the entire night away.

"Hey, babe." I stood up from the recliner, and I walked over to her bedside. "How come you didn't wake me up when you woke up? I tried my best to wait up for you. I'm so happy you're okay. Did you see the motherfucker who did this?

"All I know is that it was definitely a man. He was dressed in all black. The crazy part was that I don't remember him saying anything. It happened so damn fast. One minute I was tussling with him and the next I was on the ground."

"On my son, I'm going to find whoever the fuck did this! That's why as soon as you're well enough to fly; you're going back to Chicago. I feel better with you and the kids being out there. While I'm out here trying to get down to the bottom of this shit, I don't want my son or you out here."

By the looks on her face, I could tell that she wasn't feeling that shit.

"Cross I know you're worried about me, but I'm not going to Chicago."

"Don't fight me on this shit! Shit just got real out here in the A, and I can't have my family here." Heaven was trying to fight me at the wrong damn time. If I ever needed her cooperation, a nigga needed it right now.

"I'm not fighting you on anything. I'm staying here, Cross. What type of wife do you think I am?"

"This doesn't have anything to do with the type of wife you are. You're a great wife."

"You damn right I'm a great wife. Leaving you here alone to fight this shit would make me less than a wife. I don't know about you, but when I stood before God and agreed to better or worse, I meant that shit. I know you think I'm fragile Cross, but I'm not. You are my husband, and no matter what, if it comes down to it, I'll take a bullet for you. There ain't a doubt in my mind that you won't do the same for me. I'm not the type of wife that leaves her husband when he needs her the most. This is our fight. You can forget me going to Chicago. Now get my clothes so that I can get out of here."

I couldn't be mad at her for wanting to stand ten toes down. Running my hand over my face in frustration, I couldn't do shit but honor her request. The queen has spoken. I don't agree with the shit, but after this scare, she can have whatever she likes.

"In case you forgot you just got shot and have a concussion. The doctor wants you to stay a couple of days, and I agree. Plus, I need to find somewhere that's safe for you since you insist on staying. We can't go back to the house because we don't know where this shit came from. Promise me that you'll follow my lead. That's the least you can do since I'm not fighting with you about staying here."

"I promise, Cross. I'll follow your lead. Don't worry. Baby, you just make sure to make it back home in one piece." Heaven reached up and grabbed my face to kiss me.

I had a feeling I was going to regret letting Heaven make me change my mind. At the same time, it's imperative that I allow her to stand ten toes down if that's what she wants. Just thinking about how she put it all there about why she wasn't leaving made me a happy ass nigga. I wasn't happy because she was staying. I was happy because of her reason as to why she had to stay. That shit spoke volumes. Heaven has this sense of strength that I see underneath that soft exterior that she shows the world. My baby had just got shot and she didn't look scared at all. The average bitch would have been so scared that they would have jumped ship. Heaven has been holding out on a nigga. She's shooting guns, threatening to kill bitches, and taking bullets like a champ. This is not the beautiful pregnant woman I fell in love with at the gas station.

"Why are you staring at me like that?"

"Because you're so beautiful with the heart of a lion. I'm happy you're okay. A nigga almost lost his mind hearing something happened to you. I love you so much. I need to step out and make some calls. You need anything."

"All I need is some dick. I'm positive that would make me feel better."

"Your ass a freak. I'll see what I can do about that. Get some rest. I'll be back shortly. You have security posted at all times, so you're good."

After kissing her one last time, I headed out to make some calls. The more I thought about letting Heaven stay, I knew she needed to go back to Chicago. It wasn't that I didn't think we could ride this shit out as a team. As a man, I would never forgive myself if she lost her life behind me. I promised her father that I would protect her out here. I just failed miserably, and she doesn't understand how that makes a nigga feel. She's about to be so damn mad at for what I'm about to do. I'd rather have her mad at me than lose her. Just sitting and listening to her speak on how she needs to be by my side, lets me know I married the realest. Nothing would be real if I allowed Heaven to think she about to be on enemy lines with me. My wife looks better running her businesses and keeping the home front straight. A nigga dick gets so hard seeing her toting that damn Mac but Heaven was getting carried away with the shit.

━━━

"Thanks for coming. Now before you start going off, I just want you to know I'm sorry. I was supposed to protect your daughter and I didn't."

"Let me stop you right there. That's your wife and just you doing what you're doing lets me know you have her best interest at heart. I'm a man before I'm anything so, it's only right I respect what you're doing. Heaven is just like her hard-headed ass momma. They don't listen until it's too late. We both know she's about to be mad at both of us, but we just have to deal with it. Heaven is used to getting her way, so be prepared for the battle."

I shook my head because I already knew Heaven was about to wild out on a nigga. As soon as I hit that nigga Remy up, he hopped on his private jet and came to Atlanta.

"What you doing here, daddy? I talked to you on the phone this morning, and you said nothing about coming out here."

"I came out here to take you home. Your mother and I think it's better if you come back to Chicago. Cross needs to be focused on his family business out here. He can't think clearly on the battlefield if he's worried about you. What happened to you is cause for some bloodshed. You better believe we're out for blood. I would just rather you be back home while shit gets done.

"This some bullshit! Really, Cross? I thought we decided that I was going to stay here." Heaven rolled her eyes and folded her arms across her chest. The fact that she had her lip poked out was humorous. That shit was not going to help.

"Yes, we agreed, but I changed my mind. Ms. Bam has everything packed. We're going to get you discharged and get you the airstrip. Please don't fight me on this. Trust me. This shit hard on a nigga to be away from the one thing that keeps me sane."

"Whatever, Cross! Just get me discharged! I don't appreciate y'all ganging up on me right now." She was being so dramatic right now. Heaven was really putting on with tears and shit.

"Trust me, Heaven. This is for the best. I'm going to step outside and call your momma. Don't be hard on Cross. He's doing what's best for his family."

Once Remy left the room, I stood silent looking at Heaven. She was crying like the world had ended. She wanted me to pacify her, but I couldn't.

"If you're going to be sending me back to Chicago, the least you could do is give me some dick."

"Your pops is right outside! Chill out!"

"Well, you better put a chair up to the door or something!"

Heaven leaned over to the table next to the bed and grabbed some plastic gloves.

"Stop playing with me!"

"I'm not playing, Cross! Bring your ass over here. I need to do a nut check! Drop them drawers, my nigga."

"If I give you the dick are you going to stop making me feel bad about this shit?"

"I promise."

The last thing I wanted was for her pops to walk in on me murdering his daughter pussy. If dick would make her feel better about the shit, then who was I to deny her.

After seeing Heaven and my son off to the airport, I headed straight to see the private detective I had hired. Unbeknownst to my brothers, I had hired one to find out where the fuck Ghana was. He hadn't had any luck, and that shit bothered the fuck out of me. Where in the fuck could the bitch be hiding out at? The shit was frustrating because it never took this long to find a motherfucker. That further proved that my bitch ass father was behind it. I'm almost positive he's hiding that bitch out.

"Tell me you have some news for me, Big Mo!"

"I still don't have anything on that Ghana situation. It's like the bitch fell off the face of the earth. The shit that happened with Mrs. St. Croix was definitely plotted out. All of the lines were cut prior to her pulling up. So, it had to be someone who had been watching."

"Yeah, the security company is supposed to be trying to retrieve some of the footage from different dates in case there was some shit that would help. I thought I had the system set to save each day's footage, but it deletes after twenty-four hours. Hopefully, they can retrieve some shit. I need to know who the fuck had the balls to do this shit."

The frustration that I was feeling was getting the best of me. It was people out here trying to take the wifey and me out of our glow. We haven't even got started shitting on these people yet.

"Yeah, that shit is crazy. I'm glad she's cool, bro. I know I didn't get any information about what you wanted, but I do have something interesting to show you."

Reaching across the table, he handed me some pictures. It was pictures of Haitian Jack and Carlo Vargas. This was surprising to see, especially since we've lost our business dealings with the Vargas family. Haitian Jack and the Vargas family have beefed for years. The only thing they have in common is The St. Croix Cartel. I should have known the beef would deepen when we murked his nephew Angel. I try not to even think about that whole scene. I wouldn't wish that shit on my worst enemy. Priest was trying to put on a front like he good, but that nigga is sick. Hell, I would be sick too. Thinking of Priest, I need to check in on my big bro. He's been handling the family business but has been distant. My bro ain't been right since that shit. The shit got me looking at Rasheeda crazy, but I won't speak on it.

"Good looking, bro. You'll get your monthly deposit first thing in the morning. Thanks, Big Mo. Hit me up if anything comes your way." I dapped it up with him and headed to meet up with my brothers. They needed to see this shit.

CHAPTER NINE
RASHEEDA

LOOKING AT MY PHONE, I immediately declined the call. Priest had been calling me all day, and I refused to answer. From the moment all of this shit kicked off, we've been beefing so hard. Every time he called my phone and I answered it, he cursed my ass out. The nigga was talking about me so reckless that I had to block his ass. This is the same nigga who told me not to call his phone. He needs to keep that same energy.

It's been over a month since I moved out of our house and he's been on a rampage since. I gave the nigga the space that he requested. One thing for sure and two for certain, I love Priest, but I can't take the disrespect.

Granted that nigga did catch a nigga eating my pussy, so I deserve some of the shit he's dishing out to me. At the same time, I'm angry behind this man acting like he hasn't fucked over me. At first, I was sad and shit. I was walking around this motherfucker crying, losing sleep, and weight behind my marriage. Now I'm mad as fuck, and I can feel my petty senses tingling. Priest better leave me the fuck alone with the bullshit. This man had done me wrong the majority of the relationship. I've had to fuck so many bitches up behind this man that it makes no sense.

I forgave his ass every time and never treated him like shit. That was my fault though. By always being forgiving towards him, I taught the nigga how to treat me. In all actuality, I can't be mad at him for the things he did to me. I allowed that shit. My momma ain't never lied when she said what you allow will continue to happen. All of this shit started with him, and I finished it.

Now, don't get me wrong. I'm not gloating about the shit. In all honesty, I'm not happy about my husband catching me like that. It's embarrassing, to say the least, especially, with his brothers seeing the shit too. Ever since he caught me, it's like he hates me. That shit hurts too. It hurts me because I didn't hate him when he hurt me. I guess what I'm trying to say is I deserve some type of leniency. After everything I've put up with, I fuck up once, and it's fuck Rasheeda. It's cool though because if its fuck me, then its fuck him. The only reason I haven't spazzed out is because of my kids. The bond that they have with their father is everything. They don't need to see they momma bust their father's head to the white meat.

This thing with Priest has me out here hanging out and getting fucked up. I can't remember the last time I hung out in the hood and had so much fun. Being with Priest took me away from that other part of me that was wild and free. With him, I had to carry myself differently. Marrying into the St. Croix family came with status. Don't get me wrong. I loved the luxurious lifestyle. A bitch loved that hood life. I was born and raised in the trenches, so it was what I was familiar with. Moving into the mansions and wearing high fashion designers is what I had to adapt to. If you never grew up in the hood, you wouldn't understand.

Hearing my mother headboard hit the wall made me want to scream. Since I had been here, all her and her nigga Loc did was fuck. I'm glad the kids are gone because they could hear the shit too.

I love my momma, Rashay, lord knows I do. At the same time, I hate that she acts like she's a teenager. My momma is damn near fifty looking like she twenty -five. Rashay walking around looking like a Barbie. My momma got ass and tits for days. A couple of years ago, she went to the Dominican Republic and got snatched. Her ass was like a ghetto Pocahontas in these Atlanta streets. She is putting young hoes to shame and taking they niggas too. I'm actually happy she met Loc. He has slowed her down so much.

As I sat up with my back up against the headboard, I stared at the blank page on the laptop. This was the first time I opened it up since Priest gave it to me. With all the partying and drinking the pain away, I never thought about opening it. Today was the first day that I felt inspired to do anything outside of getting drunk. The moment I got ready to type, my phone alerted me that I had a text. I should have known it was Priest.

Mr. St. Croix: *Either you come out, or I'm about to blow that bitch up!*

Throwing on a pair of yoga shorts, I rushed to the door to see if he was outside. I could see shit right there in the foyer of the house. The door was wide open, and I could see him parked in the middle of the street. He was leaning up against his Benz with a damn rocket launcher.

"Maaaa!" I screamed, banging on my momma room door.

"What the fuck, Rasheeda?" she said as she swung the door open. She quickly closed her robe and tied it tight."

"You need to go outside and tell Priest to stop. He has a damn rocket launcher talking about he is going to blow the house up if I don't come out."

"Well, it looks like you need to pack you and your kids shit and go home. Priest is not about to burn my fucking house down. I love you and my grandbabies, but love me from your house."

"Really, ma?"

"Hell yeah! You just fucked up my nigga's nut! You ain't got to go home, but you got to get the fuck out of here! I'm not used to all this damn craziness at my house. I don't know why you're acting like you don't miss that big ass mansion."

"It's not about the house. This is about Priest and his disrespectful behavior."

"No. This is about your husband catching another nigga eating your pussy. Now let's get something straight. I don't condone what you did. Two wrongs don't make a right. I don't give a fuck if you caught that nigga balls deep in a bitch, you don't whore yourself out to prove a point. All the fuck you got out of it was a wet pussy, a broken heart, and a possible trip to divorce court. Your ass is lucky he didn't kill your ass. Go on ahead out there and see what that man wants."

"I can't believe that you're putting me out of your house."

"Well, you might as well believe it. I'm not taking any chances with his crazy ass. We both know he'll blow this bitch up. Look at his crazy ass. Remember I told you he looked like the type that would go ape shit if you gave his pussy away? That right there is ape shit. Call me when you get home. With everything happening to Heaven, I feel much better with you away from this place. Baby, this hood life is not for you anymore. Go home to that mansion and get your house in order."

My mother hugged me and rushed her ass back into her bedroom. She could care less about this maniac that was outside with a damn rocket launcher.

"What the fuck is it going to be, Rasheeda? It's hot as fuck out here, and I don't have all day."

"Well leave then, Priest! Last time I checked, I was a whore, and you didn't want me around you. I'm lost as to why you're here anyway."

"Bring your ass on, Rasheeda! I'm here to put your ass dumb ass somewhere safe. Don't get ahead of yourself thinking a nigga over on anything else but that. I hate your ass, but my kids need their mother. Now go get whatever the fuck you need before you make me nut the fuck up!"

I stood in the doorway looking at his sexy ass and thinking where the fuck did we go wrong. My husband is standing in the middle of the street threatening to blow my momma house up.

"I hate your ass too! Let's be clear. I'm only leaving due to my safety. It has nothing to do with you out here with a damn rocket launcher. You make sure you stay away from me."

"Gladly! Bring your ass on." As I packed, I realized that the threat had to be real against the family for him to do all this. Just thinking about Heaven getting shot bothers the hell out of me. She doesn't bother anybody. That added with the fact that someone came to their house had my nerves bad. So, much shit is brewing beneath the surface. This incident is about to make shit hit the fan.

"Is this another spot for your hoes?" I just had to ask as he walked around a beautiful condo in downtown Atlanta. You could see the entire city from the view.

"Not today, Rasheeda. I have a lot of shit I'm dealing with. All I'm asking is for some cooperation while I'm handling shit. You nor the kids are to leave out of this condo without me knowing. Lately, you've been out wilding trying to prove a point to me. You out of all people know how it is out here in these streets. I'm surprised that you would even put yourself or the kids out like that. Me sticking my dick in other bitches got you feeling like fuck it, huh? Let's be clear! I don't give a fuck about a hoe when it comes to my family. I'm still pissed at you, and I want to fuck you up, but there's a bigger threat out there in the streets. After seeing how fucked up Cross was behind Heaven, I don't want that for us. No matter what you're still the mother of my kids, and we have a bond."

"Well, bonds are made to be broken. Show me to my room."

I understood what he was saying but nowhere in that did it sound like he was apologetic. The nigga was actually talking like I was just a female who had his kids. This shit needed to hurry up and be over so that I can be on my way.

"Calm your ass down! What the fuck is wrong with you?"

"You're what's wrong with me?"

"Clearly you've lost your mind thinking that I'm the fucking problem. Last time that I checked, it was you on your back getting your pussy ate."

Priest walked towards me like he was going to hit me. Instead, he punched a big ass hole in the wall.

"You started this shit, Priest. You're the one that cheated on me, and I forgave you. Yes, I was fucking the nigga Angel, but it was only because I was tired of you cheating on me."

"So, you out here being a whore because I was doing wrong?"

"You started and I finished it!"

As sorry as I was for doing the shit I wasn't about to stand in front of him and do that weak shit. I needed to be as harsh and careless as he was being.

"Let's get some shit straight, Rasheeda! You have a pussy between your legs not a dick. That fact alone means you have to move differently. I don't give a fuck what I'm doing. You're too fucking classy and beautiful as a woman to be out here fucking a nigga to get back at me. Don't ever lower your standards for anybody. While you were out on revenge, that nigga was playing your stupid ass. He was using your ass as leverage against my motherfucking family! You knew we had business with the nigga, and you still fucked with him. That fuck nigga had been recording your ass every time y'all met up with your dumb ass. Did you ever stop and think about how I knew your ass was with the nigga? I'm Priest St. Croix, and my mother-fucking name holds weight! You and that fuck nigga had to know I was going to find out!

"Stop yelling at me, Priest!" This nigga was yelling and going crazy. I just knew he was going to hit my ass at any minute.

"Don't tell me to stop yelling! You need to hear this shit loud and clear. That nigga's wife found them recordings and emailed them to me. You can stand here and act like this shit not fazing you, but it should. Bitch, I got recordings of my wife doing all types of shit with a nigga! I got pictures that will humble your sneaky pussy ass. You have no idea how much I've had to pay that bitch not to put you out on social media! While you were out on your get back shit, you gave that nigga some of my power! That's why I murked his stupid ass in front of you! I made sure to cut that nigga's tongue out so that he can't eat no pussy in hell either!"

Bitch, you're breathing because I love your ass, and I know you were acting out. I might not be speaking on it, but I know I'm a big cause for a lot of shit. At the same time, no matter what I've done, it doesn't make it okay for you to go out fucking random ass niggas. I would rather you leave my ass than go fuck a nigga that I have business dealing with. If you think that shit doesn't hurt a nigga, you're more fucked up than I thought!" He pushed passed me and walked out of the condo.

"Priest!" I called out to him, but he kept walking.

For the first time, I saw hurt in his eyes. My goal was to hurt him, and now that I see it, the shit doesn't make me feel any better. I should never have fucked Angel due to their business dealings. It had the potential to ruin our family. In that moment, I thought about myself and my feelings. When I first did the shit, neither Priest nor my children crossed my mind. That's what resentment does to you. It has you so angry and in your feelings about shit that you react without thinking. All I could think about was him cheating. The bitch that knocked on my front door claiming to be pregnant was what changed me. The moment I killed her, it changed me. The nigga that I loved left me to be vulnerable too. A bitch was never supposed to be able to do some shit like that. It's obvious we're both in the wrong to some extent. I'm sorry for fucking someone close to him as far as business goes. At the same time, I'm not sorry for cheating. The nigga knows how the shit feels. He dished it out, and he can't take it.

Since I was going to be in this damn condo for some time, I decided to get settled. Jamaica had brought my kids to me, and they were doing their thing. Priest had everything in the condo that we needed from our house, which helped me to get settled in comfortably. After having a three-way conversation with Heaven and Ketura, I decided to write. I didn't have a title at the moment, but I'm positive it will come to me later. This shit I'm going through with Priest is definitely all of the inspiration I need.

For what it's worth, I hope it brings us together. My heart still skips a beat when he walks into a room. That lets me know the love is still there. We both have a lot of soul searching to do. Right now, we're both dealing with trust issues. It's going to take for us to heal from what's separated us. If it's meant for us to fix this shit, then so be it. If it's not meant to be then, I'll bow out gracefully. He has put me through too much for me to beg for forgiveness. I know I could be the bigger person but fuck that. He needs to apologize to me correctly for the chaos that he has created.

"I'm so happy you came and kidnapped me out of that prison. Saint is driving me crazy. Pull over, this damn car sickness kicking in."

As I drove, I looked out the corner of my eye at Ketura. This is the second time I have to pull over so her ass can vomit.

"Since when did you start getting car sick? You need to take a pregnancy test."

"Are you trying to be funny? You know damn well I can't have kids. I'm not about to be wasting my money on a damn pregnancy test. I'll be okay once we make it to the nail shop and I can get a bottle of water."

"I'm serious. You know I wouldn't play with you like that. At the same time, you don't get car sick so, it's strange to me, that's all. That last doctor said that miracles do happen, so maybe it's a miracle." Ketura just stared out of the window in silence. I decided just to change the subject because this one was touchy. I pray she is pregnant.

"He destroyed my life, and he just gets to live."

"What did Saint do now? "

"Compared to what my father did to me, Saint hasn't done anything."

"What did your father do?"

"He raped me from the age of five until I was fifteen. My mother knew, I know that she knew. That's why she's distant from my sister and me. My sister lives like the shit never happened, but he raped her too. At fifteen, I got pregnant and forced to get an abortion by some bitch that did the shit in her basement. That's why I can't have kids."

Ketura was crying, and I was shedding tears too. This was the first I ever heard this so it was a shock to me.

"Does Saint know about this?"

"No. How could I tell my husband that I can't have kids because my father raped and impregnated me? Saint is not the type of man that you tell something like that to. Don't you say shit either."

"I promise I won't say anything. You should tell him though. He has a right to know why his wife can't conceive. That's all you guys want with one another. I know you love Sienna, but the fact remains she didn't come from you. As your friend and your sister, I know that shit hurts you. I'm here for you if you ever want to talk about it."

After that, no more words were spoken in regards to the subject. Pulling up to the nail salon, I looked around and couldn't wait until Heaven got back. Her salon was about to put all these hoes to shame. As soon as we stepped out the car, this bitch Ketura vomited everywhere.

"Fuck getting our nails done. Bitch, I'm about to take your ass to the emergency room. You look pale as fuck. If you're not pregnant, that means something is wrong."

"No. I'll just go back to the house, and we can grab some tests on the way. Going to the hospital would be too much. Saint be clocking my ass. I'll take the tests and call you later."

Helping Ketura back into the car we headed to CVS. I planned on getting every brand of pregnancy tests for her. Ketura's ass pregnant, and I don't care what the hell she say.

About an hour later, we were sitting on the bathroom floor at the condo she and Saint were staying in.

"Why are you so sad?"

"Because I just know at any minute I'm going to wake up, and this will be a dream. I'm not happy because the shit is too good to be true. I don't want to tell Saint right now because I don't want to get his hopes up high. I'll tell him, but first I want to go to the doctor and see for sure. Thanks for doing this with me. Don't worry. I'll keep you updated. In the meantime, make shit right with my bro. I know he fucked up for a long time, but I think it's time y'all wipe the slate clean. Life is too short— niggas are walking out the door getting murdered and leaving widows behind. Saint has done so much shit to me, but I love that nigga. He's the first man that ever loved me through my pain, and he doesn't even know it. I want to be mad at Saint, but my heart won't let me. He's rough but gentle at the same time. I never knew what gentle was until I met him. All I'm saying with him I find comfort and solace even when shit is bad. I know you and Priest got a bond out of this world. Don't let your pride get in the way from what you want. We both know you love that crazy motherfucker!"

"Yeah I do, but I can't give in so quick. Priest has been on one, girl."

"Of course, he is. That motherfucker caught your pussy in another nigga's mouth!"

"Don't remind me. Let me get to the house. He's going to have a fit behind me going out. I love you, and congratulations! I can't wait to spoil my god baby." Ketura wasn't thrilled at all and she needed to be. God has blessed her, and she can't even enjoy it. Hopefully, all things go well at the doctor. Saint was going to be so happy. All he has ever wanted was a baby with Ketura. This baby is definitely a new start. I'm rooting for her marriage just like she's rooting for mine. Quiet as it is kept I want Priest and me to work as well. Ketura hit it on the head. My pride is a big part of why I haven't folded.

About an hour later, I was walking inside the condo. Priest was sitting on the couch looking at *SportsCenter*. I already knew he was mad for me leaving so he was going to ignore me.

"Where are the kids?"

"They wanted to go with my momma. You would know that had you been here instead of out in the streets."

"I wasn't out in the streets. Ketura and I met up to go to the nail shop. I'm sorry I didn't call you daddy, but being in this fucking condo all day and every day is boring.

"I understand that its boring but y'all need to stop going out. Shit is not safe right now. What part of that don't y'all get? Please, Rasheeda, start listening to a nigga!"

"Okay Priest! You don't have to do all of that yelling. The shit is not necessary!"

"Just do what the fuck I said!" He kicked over the coffee table and walked to the back of the condo." This nigga was losing his damn mind. I swear I wanted to walk out the damn door. His mood swings were starting to get the best of me. At the same time, I was wrong for leaving knowing the severity of the situation. I poured myself a glass of wine and headed to the bedroom to find Priest. He was staring out of the huge window, smoking a blunt.

"I'm sorry, Priest. You're right. I should never have left without you knowing."

"Did that nigga fuck you better than me?" I almost choked on my wine hearing him say that. Like he really said it without a care in the world.

"No Priest. He did not fuck me better than you. Besides you cheating on me with bitches, you've been a great husband. The kids or I have never wanted for anything. There is no need to feel like you are inadequate in any area when it comes down to it. I didn't love the nigga Angel. He was something to do when I was unsure of my place in your life. I admit I didn't think about anyone or the consequences. I'm not proud of this Priest. As much as I've been through with you, I still love your ass. I know that this shit bruised your ego, but what about me. All of the women over the years did something to my soul and the way that I looked at myself. Just like you worried about if that nigga fucked me better than you, I used to think the same shit. When you didn't come home, I would wonder what them hoes had out in the streets that I didn't have. I'm not perfect, and neither are you. We've both made mistakes. We're either going to forgive one another or go our separate ways. Either way is cool with me. I love you, but not enough to beg you to stay with me. I'm entitled to keep the little dignity I have left. The ball is in your court, Priest. I wave the white flag because I'm tired of fighting."

Waiting for him to respond, I leaned up against the dresser. Grabbing my glass of wine, I sipped and stared at him. He was still looking out of the window in deep thought with his stubborn ass.

"I'm sorry for whatever pain I caused you. I'm still not over this shit with that nigga, but I'll wave the white flag as well. I know I love you, and I also know I fucked up. It's just hard as a man. I guess that saying is true about niggas dishing it out but not being able to take it. Seeing that nigga eating your pussy did something to me. Shit crushed a nigga soul."

He stroked my face lovingly. That was the first time he touched me and I didn't jump. Honestly, it felt good to feel his soft hands up against my skin. It made my body react in a way that I wasn't really wanting. However, I'm in no control of what my body wants.

"What's calling it truce if there is no makeup sex?" As I spoke, I sat the glass back on the dresser and slowly removed my clothes. Stepping up in the large poster bed, I gestured for Priest to join me. No words were spoken between us as we made love with one another like it was the first time. The slate was clean, but the memory of infidelity will never fade. We just have to do the right thing by each other. I'm sure growing old together is in the cards for us. As long as he does right by me, he'll never catch my pussy in nobody's mouth but his.

CHAPTER TEN
PRIEST

NOW THAT THINGS were good on the home front, I could focus on the business at hand. As I sit looking at the pictures of Haitian Jack and Carlo Vargas, I can taste blood in my mouth. I should have known this bitch ass nigga Haitian Jack was up to no good. The nigga had been walking around like he was the man since my pops was locked up. That's why I've never agreed with my mother fucking with the nigga. He had an agenda, and he caught her when she was vulnerable. The nigga was disloyal from the jump. Any man that fucks his best friend's wife with no qualms doesn't give a fuck about shit. My pops hasn't been the best man, but he didn't deserve this nigga thinking he could take his spot. It's beyond me that he believes we would allow that shit to happen. Ma Dukes was going to be mad, but we could no longer wait and allow this fuck nigga to play with the St. Croix Cartel. With Cross and Saint on board with handling the nigga, it was no need to wait. With her being out of town, it was perfect timing to catch his ass.

"Are you sure that fat motherfucker is in there?" Saint asked as him, Cross, and I sat in an unmarked car. We had passed around two blunts, and the nigga still hadn't come out of the Caribbean restaurant.

"Hell yeah! He comes to this motherfucker every day at this time, I said flaming up blunt number three.

"Knowing that motherfucker, he's in there ordering everything off the menu." No sooner than the words left Cross' mouth, the fat nigga came out with Carlo Vargas. They shook hands and exchanged a manila envelope.

"We got action," Saint said excitedly. He had been just itching to kill somebody with his trigger happy ass.

"Look at they bitch ass! Them niggas cut out the St. Croix Cartel like the shit was sweet!" I said, taking a long pull off of the blunt.

Carlo hopped in his limo, and it pulled off. Haitian Jack headed down the street without a care in the world. I was surprised that he didn't have any security detail with him. That was a first because the nigga never went anywhere alone. Knowing him, he's cutting them out of some shit too. Saint pulled off from the curb and followed him. The moment he made it to his car, Cross and I hopped out.

"Whhh—"

"Shut the fuck up! Stop stuttering with your fat ass. Pop the trunk, bro!" Cross yelled.

"What is going on? Jamaica know y'all here doing this?" He was scared as hell. At any moment, I know he was going to shit his pants.

"She sent us." I hit his ass with so much force it knocked him unconscious. Cross and I quickly threw his ass in the trunk. The shit was a breeze.

"Please don't do this!" Haitian Jack was screaming and trying his best to squirm his way out of his fate. We had the nigga hog-tied to a roaster like he was a pig. Shooting him would be too easy. This nigga needed to suffer slowly. I think I was more mad about how he played my OG than what he did to us.

"Why should we let you go?" Saint asked as he grabbed lighter fluid and a match.

"Nooooooo!" His eyes got wide seeing Saint play with the fire.

"We should just let him go," Cross hopped in playing the good guy.

"If we let your bitch ass go, what are you going to do for us?"

"The Vargas family has shipments that come to the pier every first and fifteenth of the month."

"How do you know this?" I asked.

"Because that's who I get my bricks from now." I gestured for Saint to douse his big ass in the lighter fluid.

"Nooooo! Don't do this."

"So, you're telling me that getting bricks from the St. Croix family isn't good anymore. You and our father have been at odds with the Vargas family for years. It wasn't until we took over that Cross was able to secure their business. All of a sudden, we lose that account, and now we know why. Your snake ass has been doing side business by stepping on our toes. Now you know we can't let that shit just go."

"Your father cut me out of the business deals. What the fuck was I supposed to do?"

"We all know why that happened, so there is no need to speak on it."

"Light his ass up, bro. I'm sick of the talking." Cross stood to his feet and flicked the duck of the blunt in Haitian Jack's face. Saint started to douse him with lighting fluid. He handed the match to me, and I lit it. He went up in flames instantaneously.

"Ahhhhhhh!" He screamed and wailed as we stood watching him burn to death. We were out on the farm that we owned, and there were no neighbors for miles.

"One down! Many motherfucking more to go! Let's get the fuck out of here. These damn mosquitos are biting the fuck out of me. Mo is going to come and clean this shit up for us."

Cross walked off, and we followed behind him to the car. Haitian Jack was burnt to a crisp. The smell of his flesh burning had me sick to my stomach. I couldn't get out of there fast enough. Leaving the farm, I couldn't do shit but think about how my mother would feel bout us making a move without her knowing. She didn't care for him like we thought, but she did want to have a hand in killing him. We had to make an executive decision that she will just have to understand.

After parting ways with my brothers, I headed to the condo. My ass needed a shower. It was like I couldn't get the smell of his burning flesh out of my nose. I've killed plenty of niggas in my lifetime and this was the sickest kill ever. Leave it to Saint to win the damn coin toss on how to murk his ass.

Walking inside of the condo, I was happy to see that Rasheeda had fell asleep typing. This last week she had been working around the clock on her book. She looked cute with all the notebooks around her. Not even the drool coming down the side of her mouth took away from her beauty. How in the hell I fell in love with a Ghetto Queen, I'll never understand? There is still so much we have to work on to get back to the bond we had. Building up trust is the hardest thing to do when infidelity is involved. I didn't understand how she felt about my cheating until I was standing in her shoes. She got a nigga back, but she didn't have to get me back like that.

CHAPTER ELEVEN
JAMAICA ST. CROIX

MEN HAVE to be the stupidest motherfuckers on the face of the earth. This nigga Prentiss needs to be a spokesman for dumb niggas. Did he really think he could keep this hoe Ghana hidden? He always thought he was smarter than I was. Little did he know I was always a step ahead of him and the nigga Haitian Jack. You can't play a player.

You see I was well aware of him doing business with the Vargas family. It would only be a matter of time before my boys found out. I knew sooner or later they would catch up to his ass. When his people called looking for him, I knew they had killed his fat ass. The man really thought that I was going to go against my sons and Prentiss so that he could sit on the throne. He had to be smoking crack and fat dicks thinking that shit. I've had the man so gone behind this cougar kitty that he granted me access to all of his accounts. All of the money he made my boys lose, they got all of that shit back three times over. I play many motherfucking games but not about my kids, which leads me to where I am now. I'm sitting outside of a beautiful ass estate in Suwanee, Georgia.

Something told me to take a good look into our finances and properties. Over the years, Prentiss had purchased lots of real estate. Going through the books with my accountant, I discovered that money had been coming out of Prentiss personal accounts. With him being in jail, I had total control over all of his finances. That's how I learned about the property. I reached out to a friend down at the county building and was able to find a deed. Low and behold, the name on the deed was none other than Ghana Gilliam. This nigga had got his bitch a house, and we were paying for the shit.

I wasn't even mad about him tricking dough on the bitch. She wouldn't be the first or the last. My beef with this bitch was her thinking it was okay to shoot my son. I love all my kids, but Cross and Monae are my life. Just thinking about my baby girl, I'm glad she's away from all of this bullshit. Her husband, Ace, was the best thing that ever happened to her. He did right by taking her away from this life. Prentiss thinks otherwise, but who gives a fuck what he thinks. These days his name holds no fucking weight.

I pray he rots in the very jail that he's hiding in. That nigga is still refusing our visits. We can't even attend court proceedings. He's really on some bullshit, but it's cool though. As long as my boys have me, they don't need his ass. People like to think I'm this quiet ass woman, but my silence is deadly. This hoe Ghana thought she could out slick me. She was about to find out just how much she and Prentiss underestimated me.

Looking in the rearview mirror, I check to make sure my hat was down enough where my face couldn't be seen. Screwing the silencer on to my gun, I gripped it tightly. Grabbing the huge Edible Arrangements from the back seat, I headed up to the front door. I continuously pressed the doorbell to make the delivery look real. The damn delivery people will ring the shit out of your bell in an effort to get an answer.

"Yes! Can I help you?" Ghana answered the door like she was out of breath. The sweat dripping down her face and the wet workout clothes told me that she was working out.

"As a matter of fact, you can. I pushed her inside the door. Once she realized who I was, she tried to take off, but I let off one in her stomach. She went down like a ton of bricks. I closed the door behind me and threw the Edible Arrangements on the floor. She was trying her best to crawl away from me but she wasn't going anywhere. I kicked her over so that she was on her back. The trained hit woman looked like a weak ass bitch at the moment.

"Ahhhh!"

"Don't scream again or I'll put a bullet in your head next. Why did you shoot my son?"

"I'm not telling you shit! Take the shit up with your husband." She managed to say while she was writhing in pain. I let off a shot in each of her legs.

" Just kill me, you crazy ass bitch. I'll never tell you shit!" She tried her best to spit at me, but I jumped back.

"You don't have to tell me shit! Just know that whatever you got planned for your bastard son will never be. You see Cross, Priest, and Saint owned their place sitting on the throne. I don't give a fuck what Prentiss put in your fucking head, but the nigga lied. Your child had no stake in anything that my children have rightfully stood on the battle lines for. Just know that if that little motherfucker ever tries anything, I'm going to murder his ass. I let off a shot in her head and stood over her body for a minute.

I found great pleasure looking at the hole where her forehead once was. Stepping over her body, I caught a glimpse of a picture on the wall. It was a family portrait of her, Prentiss, and the son they shared. My heart raced a little. In that moment, I realized he felt something more for this woman than I thought. Men don't just take pictures with their side bitches and their babies for people to see. This was literally his second home. Prentiss had built a family with both of us. It was one thing for me to know about it, but to see it with my eyes was something different. If Prentiss knows what's good for him, he'll stay hiding the fuck out in prison.

CHAPTER TWELVE
SAINT

IT HAD BEEN WELL over two months and I still had my daughter. Shayla had been calling like crazy trying to get her back but I was doing the shit on my terms. I wanted to wait and see would she get her shit together. I knew if she knew when I was coming to the house it would be in order. I decided to do another pop up visit. Dealing with Shayla's nasty ass and Ketura's sneaky ass I don't know if I'm coming on going.

Lately, Ketura has been real sneaky and secretive. I know one thing if I catch her ass fucking another nigga I'm going to rip her pussy right out. I'm not Priest. I'll make sure she never pops that pussy for another nigga again. Each and every time I pull up to Shayla's spot I cringe. All of the money that I had given this hoe for our daughter was more than enough for her to move. That hoe probably spent my baby money on crack.

Without even knocking I walked inside of her house. Just like I thought the house was still nasty as fuck. Her car was outside so I knew that she was in here. As I walked down the hall I was mad that I didn't wear a damn Hazmat suit. My pretty ass was liable to get contaminated walking through this motherfucker. Glancing down at the floor I looked at a pair of panties. They were hard, stiff, and nasty as fuck. Them bitches looked like they could pick up legs and walk. This hoe panty was filled with diseases and bad fucking decisions. I should have known this hoe was nasty by the way she balled her panties up before we fucked. I can't believe I fucked this cruddy pussy ass hoe.

"Oh my God! What are you doing here Saint?" This hoe was hitting that pipe hard when I bussed inside of the room.

"What am I doing here? No, bitch what the fuck is you doing. Out of all the drugs to do you in here sucking on a damn crack pipe. No wonder you suck a mean dick. Them jaws have been putting in work. We don't even have to go through the motions. You can consider your parental rights terminated permanently! My daughter will never live with your unfit ass!"

"You can't just take my daughter Saint! I'm trying to get clean but it's so hard."

"When a beautiful little girl is involved she should be your reason for getting clean and stopping this shit. Bitch, I feel like I need to sue your crack head ass. You tricked and bamboozled a real nigga. It should be a law against that shit."

"This shit just started Saint! When I first started fucking with you I wasn't on this shit!"

"Most bitches pop pills these days but you in here smoking crack! What would make you one day decide to do crack? You know what I don't even care what your ass do at this point. Just stay the fuck away from Sienna. Ketura is her mother now."

"That is my daughter Saint! I swear to God I'm going to make you and that bitch pay for taking my daughter! Don't threaten my wife or me. Let's get something straight pussy ass hoe! Make no mistake I'll murder your crack head, crusty panty, bed bug looking ass. You're a filthy animal. You got the game fucked up if you think my daughter coming to live in fucking squalor. I'll put a bullet in your head first! Don't ever threaten me again!"

"Let me just try to get clean!"

"It's the crack that got your ass delusional. Clean is one word you will never be. Your ass had to be raised in a nasty ass house. This here is too normal for you. It's like you used to it. That bothers me. My daughter will not grow up in a house full of dysfunction. Get your shit together and maybe you can have supervised visits."

"You think that you're so better than me but you're not!"

"I am better than your crack head ass. Don't start with the soap opera theatrics and the tears. You're not in your feelings about me taking Sienna. Your ass mad because you won't be getting another dime from me!"

"I hate your ass so much! I hope they kill your ass Saint St. Croix! Just know I'm coming for my daughter. Go home and tell that barren wife of yours don't get comfortable playing mommy to my daughter. I'm coming for what the fuck belongs to me! Don't let this shit fool you. I can be as grimy as you can be."

"I doubt that bitch! You're playing Checkers hoe and I playing Chess. You not ready to fuck with me but try me. I guarantee I'll murder your entire bloodline and you know I will. Last time I shot at you I missed on purpose. Next time I intend on hitting your ass. Instead of fighting with me try fighting with a broom and some bleach. Clean this nasty ass house up. Never mind burn this hoe down. All the cleaning supplies in the world won't get this mother-fucker together!" I was done talking to the crack head bitch. I rushed getting out of that fucking apartment. My skin felt like I was breaking out in hives. A nigga had been taught a valuable lesson. These hoes out here are not real. This is God punishing me for hurting Ketura. I know I'm not the best nigga in the world but God didn't have to get me back like this. Why did he have to give me a crack head baby momma? I pay my tithes. This shit is not fair. He knows I'm too fly for this shit. That's what I get though. I already have the baddest bitch on my team! There was no need for me to be out looking for anything. I already had everything I need at home.

Walking into the house it was no shock to see Ketura reading to Sienna. Since my daughter has been living with us, she has been hands on with her care. More than I have to be honest. With running the streets and handling family business I haven't been available like I should. They deserve so much better than that from me. When all of this bullshit was over we were definitely going on a vacation.

"What happened with Shayla?" Ketura asked as she closed the book and walked over to where I stood.

"Let's just say Sienna is here with us permanently. Is that okay with you?" I had to ask her how she felt before thrusting her into adopting a child. She already has had to rearrange her life for me. The least I can do is make sure that she is okay with this shit.

"Of course I'm okay with it. That's my girl right there. That's my shopping buddy."

"I just bet the hell she is. Whose idea was it to buy a three hundred dollar head band?" Sienna started talking baby talk like she was answering my question.

"Really? How you gone throw me under the bus like that?" Ketura walked over and picked her up. Ketura kissed her on the cheek before walking her back over to where I was.

"Hey Daddy big girl!" Just looking at her I knew she needed to be with me. I don't even want to think about what she was subjected to during the time with Shayla's ass.

"There's something I need to tell you?" Ketura said as she sipped from the wine glass she was now holding. The look in her eyes kind of worried me.

"Is everything okay?" I prayed she wasn't about to tell me she was fucking another nigga.

"Yes. I just need to tell you about something that I should have been told you. Just know that I never told you because I was afraid you would look at me differently. Basically, my father raped me from the time I was five to fifteen years old. It only stopped happening because I became pregnant by him. Of course I couldn't have the baby. I was taken to this woman's house where she performed an abortion in the basement. That's why I've always said I can't have kids. As you are aware, doctors have said that having kids wouldn't be in the cards for me. Well this is why. I just never had the courage to tell you until now." I became numb listening to what she was saying. That was until she slid a gift wrapped box across the table to me.

"What's this?"

"Open it!" I opened the box and it was a positive pregnancy test. All I could do was stare it because I was lost right now.

"A couple of months ago I went to this fertility specialist. She told me that it would take a miracle for me to get pregnant. She went on to give me all types of brochures for adoption. Let's just say that positive pregnancy test is our miracle. Congratulations Saint! We're having a baby."

"You fucking with me right now!"

"No baby! This is so real. Trust me I thought the shit was a joke myself. I took twenty different tests and went to three different doctors for confirmation. I'm ten weeks pregnant."

"Come here babe!" I pulled Ketura into my embrace and hugged her. A nigga was shedding tears because this some shit that we never thought would happen for us.

"This is our miracle so we have to do everything to make sure it goes right. I don't want to speak on what I just told you happened to me. It doesn't matter anymore. The only thing that matters is building our family. Promise me you won't go after him."

"I promise." Now she knows damn well I break promises from time to time. If me telling her I promise makes her sleep better at night then so be it. I'm definitely killing him and her mammy. The bitch allowed the shit to happen.

"I can't believe this shit! You just made me the happiest nigga in the world!"

"No. You made me the happiest woman in the world. I love you so much Saint."

"I love you too Ma! Let me go call my momma and tell her. She's going to go so crazy hearing this shit." I was excited like a nigga fresh out of the joint. All I've ever wanted was a baby with my wife and now we're about to have that. I guess I'm not mad at God anymore. He made a way for us when we thought we had no way. This shit just proves how powerful prayer can be. I wanted to address the shit more in regards to how she was violated but I didn't want to stress her out at all. No matter what I'm definitely going to be getting at them motherfuckers. I'm not about to let anyone think they can do some sick as shit like that and live happily ever after. The gangster ass nigga in me couldn't live with myself if I allowed the shit to happen with no repercussions.

CHAPTER THIRTEEN
KETURA

TELLING Saint about my past was like a weight lifted off of my shoulders. Finally being able to repeat it to someone was a breath of fresh air. Over the years I never repeated it to anyone. Our family never spoke on it either. I no longer had a relationship with my mother. She chose a man over her daughters and that shit is unforgivable. Now my sister on the other hand she would rather act like the shit never happened. Her and me both know he raped us every chance he got. She's three years older than me so I an only imagine what she went through. Her ass purposely stays away from me but not today. We needed to talk about this in order to heal. The molestation and rape she endured as a child caused her to wild out as a teenager. Meeting David was the best thing that ever happened to her. That rich ass real estate mogul got my sister living the good life. I'm happy for her. Even though she gets on my last fucking nerves not liking my husband. The crazy part is that she has only met him once or twice. She has absolutely no reason to not like him. That's Kyrah for you though. Despite all of that I love her so much. Our asses has been through it and I'm so happy to be able to share my good news with her.

It's just like her to be on colored people time. I'm anxious to tell her ass I'm pregnant and she's taking all damn day. I had been sitting at Sweet Georgia Juke Joint waiting for her forever.

"I'm sorry I'm late. The traffic is crazy as hell." She rushed towards me and took a seat.

"You've been living in Georgia all your life. Your ass should have left early." Kyrah kills me acting like she doesn't know the ins and outs of Atlanta."

"Fuck all that! What the hell is so important that I come out here and the last minute? I had to cancel an important meeting with the HOA."

"Fuck the damn HOA! I called to tell you that you're going to be a auntie."

"I hope you didn't go out there adopting any damn kids. Them people come back after awhile and want their kids back."

"I didn't adopt at all. Saint and I are pregnant. It's a miracle Kyrah. I'm still in shock. Saint is so happy Sis."

"I just bet he is."

"What the fuck is that suppose to mean? Don't come in here pissing me off talking shit about my husband. Do I talk shit about David's old ass?"

"You're right. I'm sorry. It's just that I worry about you dealing with that family." Taking a sip of my peach iced tea I just stared at her judgmental ass. It was in good timing that she spoke on family. I could address the elephant in the room.

"Living life as a St. Croix is far better than that of a Billingsley. Do you ever sit back and think about what we went through in that house?"

"No Ketura! That's the last thing I think about. It's also the last thing you should be thinking about. You're living a life that you love right now and can brag about. We don't have a mother and we damn sure don't have a father. We all we got. Remember that shit. Don't be walking around letting that shit hinder you. I did for a long time. That's why right now I suffer from Depression. I don't want that shit for you. You deserve to live a happy life after what that sick bitch did to you. What he did to me I don't care about. I've always being worried about your mental headspace. I might not agree with the way Saint makes his money but I know that he makes you happy. So, that's all that matters to me. I know that I distance myself sometimes and I apologize for that. With you having this baby I plan on being all up in your business.

"Thank you so much. I swear I needed to hear that. I love you so much Kyrah." We exchanged hugs and caught up with each other. It felt good to sit and talk with her. For the first time in years we could have a conversation that didn't lead to us arguing. For so long I thought she was trying to act as if the shit didn't happen. When all she actually was doing was healing and letting that hurt go. After eating and coming up with gender reveal ideas I headed to pick up Sienna from day care. I promised Saint that I would cook him a big dinner. I hadn't fed his ass in months. Since we were on good terms I decided to be a hands on wife again.

"Hello. I'm here to pick up Sienna St. Croix." I walked up the receptionist looking for the sheet to sign her out but couldn't find it.

"Excuse me ma'am! Are you Ketura St. Croix?" An officer asked as he approached me. My heart started to race thinking something had happened to Sienna while she was in day care.

"Are you Ketura St. Croix?" He repeated.

"Yes. What's the problem officer?"

"You're under arrest for the kidnapping of Sienna St. Croix! Put your hands behind your back." He went to forcibly put my hands behind my back and I yanked away from his ass. Immediately, I was thrown to the floor face first. The shit knocked the wind out of me.

"Please! Stop! I'm pregnant!" All I could think about was my unborn baby. This man had his knee in my back and his elbow pressing down on the back of my neck. It was getting harder and harder to breathe.

"She's not resisting officer!" I heard the day care worker yell.

"Please lock her up! She kidnapped my daughter and won't give her back!" I tried my best to see where Shayla was. Her voice sounded so far away. Losing consciousness all I could do was pray this officer didn't kill me. This was not supposed to be happening. I just found out I was pregnant and in the same week I might die to police brutality. What part of the game is this? The weaker I became the more I prayed. Thoughts of my husband sank in. He was going to be so mad at me if I died on him. Hearing Shayla fake crying was agitating me. I hoped I made it because the bitch was definitely getting murked behind this shit.

CHAPTER FOURTEEN
HEAVEN

"COME ON HEAVEN. Stop crying. I promise as soon as I see what's going on back home I'll catch a flight right back out to you. Saint is going crazy threatening to blow up every damn police station in Georgia. This nigga is going to get all of us knocked. That added with still not knowing who shot you. Baby, I need to get back and handle this business. You know I'll be back before you know it. Wipe your face and tell me you love me. That shit will makes me feel so much better."

Cross was trying his best to cheer me up but it wasn't working. All I wanted to do was go home with him. Even though I'm born and raised in Chicago, home is in Atlanta with my husband.

"I love you baby. The kids and me miss you so much."

"I miss y'all too. I promise all of this shit will be over with before you know it. We're going to the South of France for an extended vacation. Plus, we still have a honeymoon we need to go on. Try not to work so hard on rebuilding the shop. I know that you want it to be back up and running. At the same time don't over do it. You're pregnant and you have to take it easy. I can't have my baby coming out all fucked up."

"Why do you keep saying that I'm pregnant?"

"When I was up in that pussy I felt that shit. That shit was wetter and warmer than usual. Had me bussing quick as hell."

"I just have good pussy! Trust and believe me I'm not pregnant."

"Yeah aight! I hope its another boy. I love you and I'll call you when my flight lands."

"I love you too. Be good!"

"I'm Cross the Boss baby! I'm always good." Cross kissed the kids that were asleep in the back seat. Before grabbing his luggage from the trunk we engaged in a passionate kiss. We didn't want to let go. The airport traffic worker was blowing the shit out of her whistle. We didn't give a fuck though. Finally, after we decided to come up for some air he walked away. I tried my best not to shed tears but it was so hard. I can't wait to get back home to Atlanta. Being here in Chicago was cool. However, it was nothing compared to going to sleep and waking up next to my husband.

As I drove away from the airport all I could do was think about Cross. The fact that he was hell bent on saying I was pregnant had me thinking. My breasts were sore and my mouth had been so watery. I was just like that with Remy Ma. I was going to be so pissed if my ass was pregnant. My baby was only six months. Between running my businesses and being the mother of two kids. I had no time for a third child right now. If I was pregnant I might as well get ready to give birth. Cross won't even be trying to hear anything about getting an abortion.

I prayed that I wasn't pregnant. My mother was going to talk so much shit. She made sure to tell me the night before I married Cross, not to let him pump me full of babies. Here I am possibly on the road to being the little old lady in the shoe.

⎯⎯

After a long ass day all I wanted to do was relax and take a nice hot bath. I could finally get a good night sleep knowing that Ketura was out of jail and the baby was okay. Unfortunately, that nutty ass Saint was in jail for terroristic threats. Shayla ass was on the run with baby Sienna. If she knows what's good for her she'll bring that baby back safe. It's crazy to find out that girl was a crack head. When I first saw her she looked well kept. She honestly was a pretty girl but that won't be for long. Long term crack use will have your ass looking like Wanda from that movie *Holiday Heart*.

I could beat Saint's ass myself. With him going to jail that meant Cross had to stay in Atlanta and try getting the psycho out. I wish I could be a fly on the wall to hear Priest cussing behind this shit. As I sank down into the hot bath water I could hear my phone ringing in the other the other room. Thinking that it could be Cross I hopped out of the tub. Rushing into the bedroom I stopped in my tracks. I closed my eyes and shook my head to make sure I wasn't seeing shit.

"It's me beautiful. Did you miss me?"

"You are not real! You are not real! You are not real!" I repeated over and over again.

"I'm very much real. Come and give your man hug." My ex Yasir who was supposed to be dead spoke as he stood up from the bed and walked towards me.

"You're dead! My man's name is Cross!" I tried yelling but he smacked the fuck out of me. I was dripping wet so I ended up losing my balance.

"Mommy!" Looking up I saw that my daughter had woke up.

"What's up Remy Ma?" He walked towards her but she made a beeline for me.

"It's okay baby. Shhh! Stop crying. Everything is going to be okay."

"I want Daddy Cross." Yasir clenched his jaws hearing her say that.

"So, you just say fuck me and take my family away from me too! Bitch, who told you to get married?" He grabbed me by my hair and dragged me across the room. That made my daughter scream and it woke my son up.

"You were dead!"

"Yeah, all your motherfuckers thought I was dead. My brother was so worried about that bitch Yah-Yah that he didn't even check to see if I was really dead. Instead he sent some whack ass clean up crew to dispose of my body. It's a good thing I did live. I've thought long and hard about just moving on with life. I can't do that without my family. You and the kids get dressed we have a flight to catch." Hearing this crazy motherfucker talk about flight I got scared.

"Look, just take me. Leave my kids here." Yasir rushed over and slapped me again. This time it was hard enough to bust my lip.

"I do not repeat myself. Get your ass up and do like I said. Wipe your face. You're too beautiful to be crying. We wouldn't even be here had you not fought me off. You would be dead!"

"You're the one who shot me?" It was all coming to me know. He was also the one who burned down my shop.

"At first I would rather see you dead than married to another man. When you survived I decided to just take his family just like he took mine. Now get dressed Heaven!"

"Where are we going?"

"To my birth country and your new home, Saudi Arabia." My heart plummeted as I heard him say that. This man was taking me to a place where men basically ran shit. I wanted to cry and scream. At the same time I needed to figure out away to leave a clue behind. My phone rang again and I tried to rush to it. Quickly, Yasir grabbed it and answered it. The way he was looking at the screen let me know it was a Face time call.

"What's good Cross the Boss?" Yasir looked like the devil.

"Who the fuck is you answering my wife phone?"

"I'm the nigga that just took your family!" Cross got ready to speak but he hung up. He laughed as he launched the phone towards the wall and it shattered into pieces!"

"Motherfucker!" I screamed as I started hitting his ass. I don't know where I found the strength to fight back. I was no match for him at all. He started beating me like I was nigga. The last thing I remembered was my babies crying and him raping me before I passed out. When I came to we were on his private plane headed to Saudi Arabia. Just like that this nigga came and snatched me away from my happily ever after!

TO BE CONTINUED

ST. CROIX CARTEL PART 2
DROPPING SOON

(SNEAK PEEK)

FOR THE LOVE OF A ST. PIERRE BOY

WRITTEN BY:
MZ.LADY P&MESHA MESH

June 1, 2017

"What's up, Dynasty? Long time no see. I bet you surprised to see me, huh?" Dot scoffed with a wicked grin, tugging at the corners of her mouth. "Yo nigga and his brothers think they the King's of the South because they got rid of Ava and Jacque, but there's a new Queen of the South, and you're looking at her." She inched toward me and pointed her gun right in my damn face, infuriating me.

As I stared down the barrel of Aunt Dot's rose gold nine-millimeter with anger soaring through my veins, all I could think about was the ways I wanted to murder her ass. It's obvious that I'm pregnant, but this bitch had no remorse for my unborn, and that was what angered me the most. If she wanted to see me, that was fine. Anytime, any place, I'm willing and ready. But damn, she could've at least waited until I dropped my load.

Wait, before I move on. Let me take you back right quick. Leilani, my A1, day one, best friend, the bitch I get mad paper with, and allat is Dot's daughter. I had to drop the aunt because she damn sure wasn't an aunt to me just like she had never been a mother to her own child. That trifling hoe had thrust my friend into the hoe game at an early age and pawned her off this balling ass nigga named June who ended up faking his own damn death. On the day he was hit up, Leilani went to the hospital only to find out he was supposedly dead and the fuck nigga was married with kids.

Everything she owned was in that nigga's name down to the club Dot had sold him, which Leilani thought was hers, and the wife, being the real fake bitch she was, made sure to throw her out on her ass. She thought she was going to get the club, but my bitch, Leilani burned that muthafucka to the ground before that hoe got to step foot on the property. That fuck shit June, Dot, and his wife was on had not only affected Leilani, but it also affected every girl who stripped at the club, including me. So, we did what real bitches do when shit gets hot, and that's put our muthafuckin heads together, and make some shake. That's how we met the infamous, muthafuckin St. Pierre Boys.

Man, life before the St. Pierre Boyz was a lot simpler than it is now. Those niggas are a rare breed. They came through and shook up our entire existence. It was bad enough that they were already fucked up, and fucking with us only made them crazier. Ava, their momma, killed their damn daddy, helped June fake his death, had their blood brother from another mother trying to kill them, and her youngest son ended up having to body her. Now, if that ain't some dysfunctional shit, then I don't know what the hell is. Mind you, all this shit popped off while we had been with those niggas. I swear, I've busted my gun so much and bodied so many niggas, you can call me a muthafuckin trooper.

Back to this bitch Dot. Man, I swear that hoe got nine lives, and she just keeps weaseling her way out of shit, but today is the day. I didn't want to have to rock Leilani's momma but fuck it. That hoe got that lil bitty ass pistol in my face like I'm a punk bitch or something. One of us wasn't going to walk out of here alive, and I knew, for a fact, I wasn't trying to die. Her ass definitely wasn't used to this gangsta shit, so he didn't come prepared. I stay ready for whatever, though. I got this gangsta shit in my blood, so I'm always prepared for whatever whenever. This back and forth shit we had going on with Dot had become too much for me. I didn't run track in school because I was too lazy for that shit, so I definitely had no time to chase a bitch or a nigga. Her life gotta end today.

With everything I had in me, I reared back and punched that bitch, trying to knock her fucking lights out, and she wasn't expecting that shit. I had hit her so damn hard, I instantly dropped her, and the gun slid across the room.

Relieving all of my aggression on that old hoe, I spoke as I kicked her repeatedly. "Because of dirty bitches like you, I got too much shit going on in my life for you to be putting a gun in my fucking face. I'm pregnant, don' fucked brothers, don't know which one is my baby daddy, and Sebastian might kill my ass if it ain't his. My god damn granny got killed, my momma was fucking with the enemy who tried to kill my nigga and me, and yo ass been in the middle of shit the whole time." I stomped that bitch bloody.

"All y'all can die. Fuck you," Dot managed to get out, surprising me. Maybe she had a little more heart than I thought.

What I do know for a fact is that all along that hoe had been on bullshit, and what was even sadder was that shit was hurting my friend. Leilani didn't deserve what this bitch had done to her, and I'm lost as to how she thought she was about to run shit. I think the fuck not.

While I continued to release my rage on that hoe, Kenyetta and I were in a fucking dilemma. Kilo, her nigga, and the bitch, Shiloh, were shot the fuck up. See, Kenyetta and I had traveled from Dallas to Chicago on a mission. Kilo had been locked up for some years, and she held that nigga down, only to find out the bitch Shiloh had been doing the same. Not only that, they had been fucking since he had been locked down and they made a baby on her. True indeed, he confessed to his sins, but he wasn't keeping it all the way gulley.

Once he got out, the nigga got down with the St. Pierre boys, so they had been living in Dallas. Then, all of a sudden, out the blue, he tells Kenyetta he had business to handle in Chicago. Now, you know us bitches be having spidey senses, so she knew that shit wasn't right. He had never mentioned any of that before.

After we followed him here, we came straight to Shiloh's house and waited for any signs of him. I wanted to kick in the door and get down to the nitty gritty, but Kenyetta was on some let's wait type of shit, so I fell asleep. But as soon as the happy family appeared, she woke my fat ass up, and we fell right off in this hoe. Those mutha-fuckas had laid the baby down and were fucking by the time we made it in the house, and all hell broke loose when Kenyetta saw that shit. She snatched his gun off the dresser and shot both they ass the fuck up.

So, now that nigga, Kilo, is coughing up blood and struggling to breathe, and Shiloh is dead as hell. Kenyetta hit that bitch with one to the back of the head, and the sight of her brains splattered on the wall behind her made my stomach churn. At any moment, I was sure my breakfast was about to come up. This pregnancy shit had me weak as fuck, and I couldn't wait for it to be over.

"Stop, bitch! What we gon' do about them," Kenyetta cried as she pulled me away from Dot.

That fast, Dot was placed on the backburner, and I was brought back to reality. While I looked on at all that carnage, my mind was running a mile a minute about what to do next.

"Give me the gun, Yetta?"

"I think I killed him, Dynasty?"

"Stop crying and give me the gun! We about to get the fuck out of here so we can get help!"

Kenyetta's ass was nervous and panicking, and about to make me shoot her ass, too. Right now wasn't the time. I needed her game face on. I wasn't one hundred percent sure about what to do with Kilo and Shiloh, but one thing I was sure on was this old bitch, Dot was not about to cause anyone else any more pain.

Once Kenyetta handed me the gun, I quickly aimed at Dot. She was laid on the floor, looking half unconscious, and was shaking like a leaf, so I knew she was scared. That was my leverage over her ass. I would buss my shit with no problem.

Before I got to put a hot one off in her, Kilo started making noises and moving around, garnering my attention, so I looked off to see if he was still alive.

"Ahhh!" Kilo screamed as he tried to get up.

"Kilo, baby! Be still don't move." Kenyetta had rushed over to him, and he had the look of death in his eyes. If he did survive, he was going to murk that bitch when he healed.

While I looked on at them, somehow Dot managed to get to her gun, and as she stood, she pointed it at me, and screamed, "You think I won't shoot your ass, Dynasty!"

Rolling my eyes, I turned back around to face her. "Damn, aren't you tired of hurting, Leilani? You want to kill us, but for what. All yo problems is because of shit your bitch ass did."

"Fuck, Leilani! She dick silly over that nigga, Luxe! All you hoes brainwashed!"

"Like how Ava had you brainwashed! It's funny how now you talking like you the big bad boss when just a minute ago Ava had you on your knees force feeding you her pussy! You can miss me with this tough ass act you putting on. Let's play make a deal. I'll pay you whatever money that's owed to you so we can get him to the hospital and you can live for now, or I kill yo ass, and you get nothing."

And so the plot thickens. While Kilo was locked up, Kenyetta started messing with a trick ass nigga named Big Fred, and he was really looking out for my girl. Kilo got wind of it and killed the nigga after busting them together, and they ran off with two million of his dollars. Come to find out, the nigga Big Fred was Dot's brother, and now she wants revenge. Go fucking figure after all she's done to people.

"Do it look like I make deals with the help?" That bitch laughed, triggering something inside of me.

"Nah, pussy ass hoe! You the help, and I'm the Devil!" I pulled the trigger until it jammed.

Dot slumped to the floor with a loud thud and was dead before she even knew what had hit her. After hearing her big ass body fall, it brought me back to our other situation.

"What are we going to do now?" Kenyetta cried as she paced back and forth.

"Shut the fuck up and let me think!"

"He's not moving anymore, Dynasty!" While she was crying, the little girl that was previously asleep on the couch was standing in the doorway in shock. I had forgotten all about her ass, but I couldn't give her much thought at the moment.

While accessing everything around me, an idea came to my head.

"Yetta, call the police and tell them you came to see your brother and found bodies in the house. Along with your niece, crying, and she was all alone. Do it while you move the car up the street that we came in. It can't be parked out there because they'll make it a part of the crime scene. We don't need that. I'll set the scene in here. And stop looking like that. I'll handle everything. If you're going to be a part of this crew, then you need to toughen the fuck up! All of this scared and nervous shit will get us knocked!" I chastised.

Kenyatta was frightened out of her mind, and I was too because Kilo didn't look too good. The scene before me was all fucked up, and I had a matter of minutes before the police would be pulling up. After placing the guns strategically to make it look like a damn shootout. I wiped off anything I thought we touched and waited outside with the little girl who looked just like Kilo's ass. Both Kenyetta and I stood out front, crying like we were crazy just to give off the effect that we were distraught. And when the laws pulled up, we really put on a show to remember. We did so good with our act that after the police questioned us, we were quickly let go. Shit, that was the easy part. The hard part would be telling Diamond and Leilani what the fuck happened.

2019- Present Day

"Bitch, don't you think it's bout time you bring your ass home? Sebastian is going crazy, looking for you. Neither he nor Marcell knows what's going on with the baby, and it's hectic around these parts. Those niggas can't even be in the room together without some shit popping off, and my nigga's ready to send a search party for your ass his damn self. I love you and all, but I don't know how much longer I can pretend like I ain't heard from you. Plus, I miss my friend," Leilani sigh as she fussed at me over the phone.

Every time I spoke with Leilani, she had me feeling like a piece of shit for burning off the way I did, but I had to. For the sake of my sanity and my baby's health, I had to get far away from both Sebastian and Marcell. They were driving me crazy. Sebastian treated me like I was shit because I fucked his brother, but he pushed me into the arms of another man by cheating with his ex-girlfriend, and it wasn't like I knew they were family, anyway.

When I met Marcell, he was gunning for the brothers. He was raised by Ava's side of the family, the Baptiste, and she had it drilled in his head that they were the enemies. It wasn't until Luxe, Sebastian, and Judah were kidnapped and took to Haiti but their grandfather, that the truth came out that he was an actual St. Pierre boy. Marcell's mother was a maid for the St. Pierre family, and she and their father was in love.

For years, the Baptiste and the St. Pierre's were at war, and when they finally came to a treaty, one of the promises was that the two families unite were to unite.

They were set to be married, and their bloodlines would live on through the children. United, the two families would become the most powerful people in all of Haiti, and the Baptiste was looking forward to that, especially Ava. When she got wind of the relationship between the father and the love of his life, she killed her, cut out her baby. She took him home to the Baptiste, and they were the ones who had raised him, so he believed that he was one of them.

Long story short, Marcell used me. He knew exactly my man, and I was. I was so vulnerable at the time because of all the things going on between Sebastian and me, so that made his job even easier. I will admit, though, Marcell was a breath of fresh air after what I had been through. He was kind, fucked the dog shit out of me, handsome, attentive, and always at my beck and call when I needed him. Had he not been related to Sebastian, I can't say who I would've been with right now. I love Sebastian wholeheartedly, but I care about Marcell, too. I'm so damn confused.

"I want to come home, but I don't know what the hell I'll be coming home to, and I'm a mother now, Leilani. If Sebastian kills me, my baby will be out here without a mother, and I don't need nobody else raising my child. Fuck all that, coming home just ain't worth it," I replied, sounding like the coward I was.

The thought of going back to Dallas to face Sebastian was so disheartening, but I knew I couldn't stay in Chicago forever. My friends and family needed me as much as I needed them. However, I was too afraid to confront the mess I'd created head on. "You make it sound like she's not Sebastian's baby. Come on now. What's really good, D?"

For a brief moment, I paused, gazing down at my one-year-old daughter, Cherish, unsure of how I would answer Leilani's question. It had been a while since she was first born, so she's definitely grown into herself. However, she looked so much like me, and since Sebastian and Marcell favor one another a lot, I still was unable to tell which one was her father.

"I still don't know, Leilani," I sighed. "She looks like all three of us."

Leilani sucked her teeth. "Well, that's all the more reason to bring yo ass back. You have been keeping them from the fellas long enough, so it's time to put on your big girl panties. Besides, it's Judah and Diamond's anniversary, and they're renewing their vows. If you're not here, we will hunt yo ass down, so I'll see you in a few days. Kiss my God baby for me, and I'll holla at your ornery ass," she said before clicking the line in my face.

After sitting the phone on the dresser, I stood from my bed and stretched, then headed to the restroom to shower while Cherish still slept. Upon entering the restroom, thick, steamy fog smacked me in my face, and I smiled at the outline of the dark chocolate silhouette taking residency in my shower. Dropping my robe to the floor, I unveiled my naked body and pulled the shower door back.

"You feel like washing my back?" I asked my boo flirtatiously as I stepped in the shower behind him.

He grinned, turning around to face me, then backed me into the wall. Grabbing hold of my legs, he lifted me off my feet and guided himself inside of me as he replied, "I'll wash yo back, but I'm about to fuck the shit out of you first. Bust that pussy open for me, baby," Marcell demanded, making things a lot harder for me than they should be.

SUBMISSIONS

**To submit your manuscript to Shan Presents, please
send the first three chapters and synopsis
to submissions@shanpresents.com**

CPSIA information can be obtained
at www.ICGtesting.com
Printed in the USA
BVHW031827100719
553110BV00001B/19/P